Rescued by a SEAL

AN ALPHA SEALS NOVEL

Makenna Jameison

This book is a work of fiction. Names, characters, places, and incidents are the product of the author's imagination. Any resemblance to actual events, locales, or persons, living or dead, is coincidental.

Copyright © 2019 by Makenna Jameison

All rights reserved, including the right of reproduction in whole or in part in any form.

ISBN: 9781798488638

ALSO BY MAKENNA JAMEISON

ALPHA SEALS

SEAL the Deal
SEALED with a Kiss
A SEAL's Surrender
A SEAL's Seduction
The SEAL Next Door
Protected by a SEAL
Loved by a SEAL
Tempted by a SEAL
Married to a SEAL
Seduced by a SEAL
Rescued by a SEAL

SOLDIER SERIES

Christmas with a Soldier
Valentine from a Soldier
In the Arms of a Soldier
Return of a Soldier
Summer with a Soldier

Table of Contents

Chapter 1	1
Chapter 2	14
Chapter 3	25
Chapter 4	36
Chapter 5	54
Chapter 6	59
Chapter 7	68
Chapter 8	79
Chapter 9	92
Chapter 10	109
Chapter 11	123
Chapter 12	130
Chapter 13	139
Chapter 14	150
Chapter 15	157
Chapter 16	166
Chapter 17	175
Chapter 18	184
Author's Note	191
About the Author	193

Chapter 1

Mason "Riptide" Ryan jumped and shot the basketball from the three-point line, listening to the "swoosh" of the ball as it sunk into the net after sailing through the air. He smoothly landed back on the blacktop and swiped his brow with his forearm.

Nothing like an outside game of hoops on a gorgeous evening, the salty ocean air from a few blocks away blowing around them.

"Whoo-hoo, sailor!" a woman from a group hanging outside the fence of the basketball court shouted. "You can sink into me anytime!"

"Becky!" her friend admonished, shushing her.

Mason smirked as the two women walked away, sashaying in their skimpy shorts and tank tops. He and his teammates were playing on a court at the edge of base, where some of the local women were known to congregate in hopes of catching a glimpse of the Navy SEALs.

And vice versa.

Nothing wrong with playing ball with his buddies while he had a few attractive women cheering them on.

He watched the hips of the woman who'd shouted at him temptingly sway back and forth as she and her friend moved toward a row of men jogging around the perimeter, pausing to smile and wave at the young recruits.

Her short shorts barely covered her ass.

Hell.

Those type of women didn't seem to care whose bed they ended up in—as long as it was the bed of a military man.

He'd been all about those types in his younger days but just didn't find them as tempting lately.

Didn't mean the younger guys weren't happy to take them home for the night though.

"Three points!" his team member Noah "Viper" Miller shouted, clapping him on the back. "You boys owe us a round of beers."

Mason chuckled, glancing over at the two other members of their Navy SEAL team across the blacktop. "Anytime you guys wanna pay up works for me," he said with a grin. "I could go for a couple of beers."

"Hell, you just want to see Taylor again," Jacob "Joker" Olson said, bending down to grab the basketball that had rolled to the edge of the court. He easily palmed it with one large hand, glancing up as the roar of twin jet engines temporarily drowned them out, two F-15s from the nearby naval air station flying across the sky.

"Affirmative," Mason said. "Not that I've

convinced her to go out with me yet."

"She got any friends?" Jacob asked.

"The hell if I know," Mason replied, sauntering toward one of the buildings on base as the rest of the men followed behind him. "She barely said a word the last time we were at Anchors. Usually she'll hang out for a bit even if she's working. Take her time passing out drinks and grub so we can flirt a little."

Anchors, a popular bar on the Virginia Beach oceanfront, wasn't far from their Navy base at Little Creek. It was always filled with single military men and local women, both looking for a good time, but Mason had taken interest in one of the waitresses there in particular.

And his teammates had clearly noticed.

He imagined the flush that always spread across Taylor's face as he teased her when he was there with his buddies, that dark brown ponytail swinging back and forth as she moved around the bar, and those chocolate brown eyes warming up every time she looked at him.

Ryker "Bulls Eye" Fletcher raised his eyebrows, his gray eyes flashing. "Think everything's okay?"

"Dunno," Mason grunted, stalking toward the door. "She gave me her number a few weeks ago but has been busy every time I've asked her out."

"Crash and burn," Jacob said with a howl of laughter. "Guess she wasn't interested after all."

"Hell, it feels like it," Mason said, pulling open the door and flashing his ID. "I haven't seen much of her since we got back from Bogota. Maybe she thought I was blowing her off by not showing up at the bar like usual."

"She knows you're a SEAL," Ryker said. "Taylor

knows the drill. We disappear for a while and then come back. Same with half of the other guys in Anchors. No harm, no foul."

Mason shrugged as they moved toward the locker room. "Something still feels off. She was always flirty in her texts before—flirty yet unavailable, I might add."

"Shit, you've been texting her? Was she sending you fucking heart emojis or something?" Ryker asked with a chuckle.

"Very funny, jackass," Mason said as he opened his locker. He pulled his sweaty tee shirt up over his head, ready to hit the showers.

"Man," Jacob muttered beside him. "First Hunter and Colton find women of their own, and now you, too? Maybe the Delta team can have a triple wedding or something."

Their SEAL team leader Hunter "Hook" Murdock had met his girlfriend Emma in London while on the run from terrorists. Colton "C-4" Ferguson had met Camila as part of their op to take down her father, a notorious drug lord in Bogota. Neither of the SEALs had expected to fall for the women they'd rescued, but both Emma and Camila had moved to Virginia Beach and seemed happy as hell to be with their men.

And Colton and Hunter were now very much absent from their evening games of basketball and nights out at Anchors.

"I'm not with Taylor," Mason said. "I like her—so shoot me. She's gorgeous, and it's cute as hell the way she always blushes around me. That doesn't mean I'm going to marry the woman or something. Hell, I haven't even taken her out yet."

Ryker snickered, stripping off his own shirt. He

balled it up and tossed it aside. "Bang her first, bro. No need to rush into marriage."

Mason muttered to himself, slamming his locker shut. The rest of his SEAL team was single and more than happy to play the field. To take home a different woman every week. What the hell did he expect? If a woman they were interested in wasn't readily available, they moved on to the next good-looking chick to come by.

No harm, no foul.

Why was he so hung up on Taylor anyway?

If she'd thrown herself at him and begged him to take her home for the night, would the thrill of the chase be gone?

It wasn't that though, he rationalized. She was different than the type of women he usually went after. More reserved. Quieter. Shy.

But something about the way she always looked at him thrilled him to no end.

If she blushed that much just from being near him, he'd love to see how she reacted if he bent over and stole a kiss. Pulled her down on the sofa at his place and made out with her.

Took her to bed and enjoyed her for hours.

"Hell," Noah said, stopping beside him, gripping his towel around his waist as he headed for the showers. "Just ask her if everything's okay. Women like that shit."

"And suddenly you're an expert on women," Mason chuckled.

"The last woman I took home didn't have any complaints," Noah quipped.

Mason smirked as his buddy walked off. Damn it all to hell. It wasn't his place to worry about Taylor, a woman he for all intents and purposes barely knew.

They were acquaintances, barely. Not friends. Not dating. Not lovers.

He had a nagging feeling something wasn't exactly right though. And as a Navy SEAL, he'd been trained to follow his instincts. To be aware and observant at all times.

The question was, even if something was going on in Taylor's life, they were practically strangers. A few texts and flirty dinners where she waited on their table weren't exactly the start of a relationship.

Would she even want his help?

***

Thirty minutes later, Mason was driving down the highway from Little Creek toward Virginia Beach. His stereo blasted through his SUV, and the ocean breeze blew in through his open windows.

He passed a couple of large high-rise hotels, aiming for the parking garage close to Anchors.

They were at Uncle Sam's beck and call 24/7. Getting called on a mission meant they were wheels up within hours. Most of his team was still single, and they enjoyed nights out when they were all stateside. Hell, the other SEAL team stationed at Little Creek, the Alpha SEALs, were all married or in a serious relationship. A couple of them had kids already.

Mason pulled into a parking garage along Atlantic Avenue, the long stretch of road that ran along the busy section of Virginia Beach. He hopped out of his SUV, setting the alarm before crossing the dimly lit garage and walking down the block toward Anchors.

A gentle breeze blew in from the ocean. His gaze

swept the area on the boardwalk—although there were a few people strolling along the water, it was nothing like the summer months when tourists flocked to the area.

He pulled open the door to the popular bar, the sounds of music and laughter and scent of fries and burgers hitting him. A long bar stretched across one side of the restaurant, but his gaze landed on their usual spot.

Hunter and Emma were already nestled at a table at the back, Emma sitting comfortably on Hunter's lap. Hunter lifted his chin in greeting as he saw Mason, his arms wrapped around his woman.

His tattoo peeked out beneath his shirt sleeve, the scruff of his beard just beginning to look shaggy, and Mason smirked at how different Hunter and his Ph.D. girlfriend were. If they weren't an example of opposites attracting, he didn't know what was.

"Where's everyone else?" Hunter asked.

"Must be busy doing their make-up or something," Mason quipped, sinking into a seat.

Emma burst into laughter, brushing her red hair off of her face. "Brilliant," she said in her British accent. "I'd love to see them in some lipstick and rouge."

"Rouge?" Mason asked, wrinkling his brow.

"The hell if I know," Hunter said, taking a pull of his beer. "Apparently it's all the rage in London."

"I'd look as white as a ghost without any makeup on," Emma chided him. "I've got fair skin that needs all the help it can get."

"You look perfect," Hunter corrected her, taking her smaller hand in his and kissing the back of it. "Gorgeous."

"Keep it in your pants, Hook," Mason said, calling him by his nickname.

Hunter guffawed as Emma's cheeks turned a rosy shade.

"Easy, princess. Mason just hasn't gotten laid in a while."

Mason chuckled as Emma shushed her boyfriend.

Hell.

Mason had been there at the London pub when Emma and Hunter had first met. The chemistry between them had sizzled right from the start. From the looks of things, it hadn't fizzled out at all since she'd moved here. If anything, Hunter was even more sickeningly sweet toward her.

Hunter.

One of the biggest, baddest dudes on their SEAL team, brought to his knees by a British chick.

"What's so funny?" Hunter asked.

"I see who wears the pants in your relationship. Emma looks like she calls all the shots. She's got you wrapped around her finger."

"Thank you," Emma said. "I always knew I liked you, Mason. Handsome and intelligent."

"Hey," Hunter said in a low voice, nuzzling her neck as she squirmed. "Don't make me jealous over here."

"Over here?" Emma asked with a laugh. "I'm literally on top of you. How could you be jealous?"

Hunter raised his eyebrows. "On top of me? Hell, I like the sound of that."

Emma blushed furiously as Mason guffawed.

Noah, Jacob, and Ryker walked in together just then, sauntering toward the back. Emma's gaze fell on Noah, her lips quirking in amusement. "I think your aviators are glued to your head. I've never seen you without them."

The men all chuckled as Noah grinned. "They do seem to attract the ladies. And don't worry—I make sure to take them off when I have a woman in my bed. Can't have them falling off during sex."

Hunter growled from his seat. "She wasn't worried—and she sure as hell wasn't thinking about you having sex."

Noah smirked. "That makes one of us. I'm already hoping to find a beautiful woman to bring home with me for the night. Just have to decide who the lucky lady is."

"Well, it sure as hell isn't your looks that draws the ladies in," Ryker said, grabbing a chair and sinking backwards onto it. "Hunter, Emma," he said, nodding at the couple.

"Where's the waitress?" Jacob asked, glancing around. "Is Taylor here tonight?"

Hunter shook his head, his eyes sweeping toward Mason. "I haven't seen her the last couple of times we've been here."

Mason frowned. "Me either. I was just saying earlier that something seems off with her. She used to be working practically every night, and she's hardly around anymore."

A young, blonde waitress walked over to their table, notepad in hand. "What can I get you boys tonight?" she asked, her pink lips shining with some type of lip gloss. Her gaze raked over Ryker, and Mason smirked.

"How about your phone number?" Noah teased.

She batted her heavily made-up eyes at him. "I'm not sure if you're my type," she teased him.

"Well, you're certainly mine," he quipped.

Hunter's gaze swept from Noah to their waitress. "A round of beers for everyone. On me. We're celebrating tonight."

"Hoorah!" Noah said with a grin.

"Hell," Ryker said as the blonde waitress walked away. "Colton and Camila aren't even here yet."

"So we'll order them a round when they get here," Hunter said. "No reason we can't get started."

"Hey fellas," a voice drawled, and Mason glanced over to see Matthew "Gator" Murphy walking over with Brent "Cobra" Rollins. The two men were on the Alpha SEAL team at Little Creek. Both the Alpha and Delta teams worked together at times, deploying jointly on missions. The Delta team had just gotten back from Colombia though while the Alpha team had been in the Middle East.

"Where's your better halves?" Jacob asked.

Brent smirked at them. "Ella's busy taking a class. She's actually going to graduate early in December but wants to get her Master's Degree after that. She was accepted to a graduate program here."

"Hell, that's awesome, man," Mason said, nodding at the other SEAL. "To transfer schools and finish early is pretty sweet. And grad school, too? Fantastic."

Brent had met Ella down in Florida. He'd come to her rescue when her sleazy boss at the cocktail lounge where she worked had pawned her off on some men he owed money to. Ella had ended up moving to Virginia Beach to finish college here.

Such was the life of a SEAL. They went where the U.S. Navy sent them—and their wives or girlfriends had to come along, for better or worse.

"Yep. I was looking forward to seeing more of

her," Brent said. "She was planning to get a job after graduating, but it looks like now she'll be spending more of her nights studying and writing papers. She's more serious about school than I ever was," he added with a chuckle.

"Bri's at home with the baby," Matthew said. "I did daddy duty the other night while some of the women went out. Now it's my turn to have a breather. Man, that little fella can scream."

"Shit," Hunter said as Emma stood and headed off to the ladies' room. "You boys could open a goddamn daycare with all the kids you have."

"Not me," Brent said. "I don't know a damn thing about babies. Nor do I want to."

Hunter chuckled. "And what does Ella say about that?" he asked, crossing his arms as he leaned back in the chair, his mouth quirked up in a smile.

Brent shrugged. "She's busy with school now—no time for a kid."

"But grad school won't last forever," Mason needlessly pointed out. "Give it a few years, bro."

"We're meeting some of the other guys here," Matthew drawled.

"Well hell, pull up a chair and join us," Hunter said. "We're celebrating our latest successful op."

"Another time," Matthew promised. He and Brent headed off to the bar area to wait for the rest of their team, and the blonde waitress sashayed back over, holding a heavy tray of drinks.

Mason's gaze landed on her name tag. "Emily," he said, watching as her eyes flicked over to him. "Have you seen Taylor around?"

"She called out again," Emily said with a wry smile, handing out the bottles of beer to the guys.

"Called out as in she's sick?" Mason asked, his eyes narrowing.

"I'm not sure," Emily said. "She's missed several of her shifts. She was sick a couple of weeks ago, but I'm not sure why she hasn't been around lately."

"Is she having car trouble again?" Mason asked. The last time the team had been in here, she'd told him how she'd paid $400 for a tow. Mason had wanted to wring the neck of the tow truck driver who'd taken advantage of a single woman. Hell, he'd have changed her damn tire himself. Now that he had her number, and vice versa, he'd hoped she'd be in contact with him more. After a string of flirty texts though, he'd disappeared with his team to Bogota a couple of weeks ago.

And he'd barely gotten a response back from her since.

Emma walked back over, her red hair swishing around her. "Camila just texted me—she and Colton are on their way."

"About damn time," Jacob said with a grin. "Why do you think they were running late? Maybe they needed some extra time between the sheets?" he asked, waggling his eyebrows.

"Hush," Emma chided him. "She just moved here. Of course they're going to be enjoying their time alone."

"Poor old Colt is pussy-whipped," Noah said, taking a swig of his beer.

Emma reached over and lightly smacked him on the arm as Hunter guffawed in amusement.

"He's pretty damn happy," Mason said, taking a pull of his beer.

"Says the guy who's been hung up on a woman for

months," Noah said.

Mason shrugged. "She knows I'm interested in her. Hell, how many times have I asked her out now? It's not exactly a state secret. First she said she didn't date customers, then that she wanted to take it slow. She gave me her number though."

"You should ring her up," Emma said in her British accent. "You have her mobile—why keep texting when you could just ask her out on a proper date?"

"I have asked her out," Mason said. "A couple of times. But you're right. I'll give her a call this weekend now that we're back in town. If she's not interested, I can take it," he said with a shrug. "But then I'll at least have an answer."

"Bravo," Emma said, as the men chuckled.

Mason scanned the restaurant out of habit, hoping Taylor would somehow appear out of thin air. The waitresses working tonight were busy, carrying full trays between tables. But as their own waitress had already said, Taylor wasn't there.

Again.

Mason clenched his jaw, reaching for his cell phone.

Chapter 2

Taylor Reynolds frowned as she scanned her small apartment, the evening sunlight coming in through the slatted blinds on her balcony door. A burst of salty ocean air blew into the living room, and she crossed the room, pulling the window beside it shut.

The click of the lock felt like it sealed her fate.

She was stuck inside here for the night. Figuratively at least.

Her stack of books and empty mug were in their regular spot on the coffee table, her camera right beside them. Her jacket and purse tossed onto the arm chair, ready for her to grab before heading into work.

And her ex-boyfriend lay sprawled across her sofa, passed out in another drunken stupor.

Her gaze narrowed. His large frame took up all three sofa cushions, and although at one time she'd been attracted to his muscular, athletic build, now it just intimidated her.

Eric had been showing up more and more lately, and she was starting to feel jittery any time someone knocked on her door, fearful that it was him. Afraid that he'd come by and refuse to leave. Refuse to let *her* leave.

She couldn't go into work late and just leave him there in her apartment—he'd be furious if he woke up and she was gone.

Not that she should have answered the door in the first place.

But if she sent him away, drunk, who knows what would happen. She hoped to God he hadn't driven over here, but she couldn't exactly send him on his way knowing that he'd be on the road with other drivers. Knowing that he could hurt—kill—someone else. Someone innocent.

She stiffened, inhaling sharply as memories washed over her. Of a drunk driver crashing into her sister's old Toyota Camry. Of rushing to the hospital to wait with her parents, hoping and praying for a miracle before they finally had to take her off life support.

As much as she detested Eric's behavior, she couldn't in good conscience just send him on his way. She hadn't wanted to let him in, but she knew he'd be furious if she left. It was easier just to call out from work and wait for him to wake up sober. Again.

She'd remind him that they broke up and send him on his way, hoping he finally got it.

Panic rocketed through her as she heard someone in the hallway, and she realized she'd forgotten to text her best friend to cancel her ride. Hurrying toward her front door, she quietly edged it open. She couldn't exactly play sick since she was dressed and ready to go—makeup on, hair neatly pulled back into a ponytail, Anchors tee shirt worn over her jeans.

Bailey frowned as she saw the expression on Taylor's face. "What's wrong?" she immediately asked. "Are you okay?"

"I'm so sorry," Taylor gushed, "but I forgot to text you. I'm not going into work tonight after all."

Bailey raised her eyebrows, her blue eyes sparking. Her knowing gaze slid to the door. "What? Why not? Are you sick or something?"

Taylor stepped into the hallway, pulling the door behind her. After she quietly eased it shut, she met her friend's gaze, her heart hammering in her chest. "Eric showed up," she whispered. "He reeked of alcohol—he must've been drinking all day long. I don't even know how he got here—I'm really hoping he didn't drive over to my place. But I can't just leave him here all alone."

Bailey's gaze landed on the closed door. Her blue eyes tracked back to Taylor. "And you let that asshole in? What's he doing now?" she whispered furiously.

"Passed out drunk on the sofa."

"Well, come on. I'll drop you off at work, and you can crash at my place tonight. He won't stick around here forever. Just let him sleep it off. And the next time he shows up, don't open the door. Don't even go near the door—just call the cops and be done with it. They can arrest him for being drunk in public or something. Maybe a night in jail would sober him up quick. Seriously Taylor—he's bad news."

"No," Taylor said, shaking her head as her ponytail bobbed back and forth. "I can't leave. He'd be furious if he wakes up and I'm not here."

"He's passed out drunk! He won't remember if

you told him you were leaving. Besides, you guys broke up. He shouldn't even be coming over here at all. Ever. Who cares if he's mad? He certainly doesn't have a say in whether or not you go into work. Tell him to fuck off and screw up someone else's life."

Taylor let out a sigh. "It's not that simple."

"It is."

Taylor helplessly shrugged. "He always apologizes when he's sober—says that he needs someone to talk to. I mean, I guess he just hasn't gotten over things yet. I'm the one that called it off. And his drinking so much might be a cry for help."

"So what? People break up all the time. People get divorced more quickly than your break up. Go. Get your stuff. You can't just let him keep controlling your life. Let his friends and his family deal with him. Eric is not your problem anymore. How many days of work have you missed anyway?"

"A lot," Taylor admitted. "I was sick a few weeks ago, so I missed a couple of shifts then. But now Eric is showing up at my apartment all the time, saying we need to talk again."

"He's manipulating you—you know that, right? And I'm worried. He might be passed out drunk now, but what about when he turns into an angry drunk? Or an abusive drunk? You need him gone. You sure as hell don't need him in your apartment."

"I know, I know. I just felt like I had to let him stay here. He barged in as soon as I opened the door and—"

"Get your stuff—we can talk on the way there."

"All right," Taylor nervously agreed. "Hold the door open for me—I don't want it to slam shut and wake him up."

Bailey raised her eyebrows, and Taylor realized how silly she sounded. This was her apartment. She could come and go as she wanted. Slam the door if she wanted. Since when had she let Eric control so many aspects of her life?

She hurried inside to grab her purse, casting one last glance at her ex.

Ten minutes later the girls were breezing down Atlantic Avenue in Bailey's convertible, heading toward the popular touristy section of Virginia Beach. Bailey slid her sunglasses on, her tiny eyebrow ring gleaming in the sunlight.

Taylor had her ears pierced but nothing else. Eric hadn't liked piercings or tattoos on women, and she'd wanted to look good for him. He'd instantly shot down her desire to get a small heart tattoo on her hip with her sister's initials in it.

Tessa had been her best friend. Only a year apart, they'd been inseparable in high school. No one would've been able to see the tattoo, save for her and Eric, but he'd insisted he didn't like them on women, especially on his girlfriend.

Maybe now that they'd broken-up, she'd go to the tattoo parlor. She wasn't generally into tattoos, and had no desire to get more than one, but something permanent to memorialize her sister called to her. Taylor's entire life had changed that day her sister's life had been taken. And the fact that she'd be doing it in defiance to her ex made her even more determined to see it through. She was done with Eric controlling her life. It was time to finally start living hers again.

She'd finally broken up with him a month ago after dating for several years when his drinking and controlling behavior had just gotten to be too much.

Who was she kidding though?

Their relationship had taken a turn for the worse months ago. The writing had been on the wall for everyone but Eric it seemed.

Grabbing her cell phone from her purse to let her manager know she'd be in tonight after all, she saw a text from Mason, one of the military guys who hung out at Anchors all the time. They'd flirted a little, harmlessly, and at one point she'd given him her number. Although they'd texted a bit, now that Eric had been showing up more and more frequently, she'd tried to ease back on the flirty texts.

There'd be no telling what would happen if Eric saw them.

Bailey glanced over at her, her blonde hair streaming in the wind. "What are you smiling about?" she teased as Taylor thumbed a response to Mason on her phone.

"Remember that guy I told you about? The one who comes in with his buddies to Anchors all the time?"

"The Navy SEAL hottie," Bailey confirmed.

Taylor blushed, her face flaming. "He texted me to say that he's there with his friends now and misses my smile."

"You should go out with him," Bailey declared. "Hell, even if you don't like him, go out with him. Just so that Eric sees a big, strong guy at your place. Maybe then he'll stop trying to push you around."

"He doesn't push me around," Taylor protested.

The car pulled to a stop at a red light, and Taylor watched the groups of people walking down the sidewalk of Atlantic Avenue. It was a perfect autumn evening. The summer crowds that visited Virginia Beach had died down, so it was mostly locals enjoying the bars and restaurants that dotted the strand.

Taylor loved spending afternoons basking in the sun, listening to the sound of the waves crashing on the shore. Some of her old friends from high school and college wondered why she was still working as a waitress at Anchors, but honestly? She loved the freedom.

A night job that paid well with decent tips left her days free for enjoying the beach. Even in the cooler months, she'd walk down the boardwalk, taking photo after photo of the ocean and enjoying the saltwater and sand.

Bailey tucked a strand of blonde hair behind her ear before admonishing Taylor, the tiny row of studs in Bailey's ear glimmering in the sunlight. "Maybe Eric doesn't push you around physically—yet. That could always change. But emotionally he sure yanks you the hell around. He's controlling, manipulative, possessive—"

Taylor burst into laughter. "Tell me how you really feel." The car pulled forward again as the light changed to green, and Taylor inhaled the salty ocean air before glancing back at her best friend. "I mean, yes, he's a jerk," she continued. "That's why I broke up with him. I don't want him to go and do something crazy though."

"Like barge into your apartment and refuse to leave?" Bailey asked drily. "And what happened with your car anyway? I thought you were getting it fixed?"

"Eric has a buddy that owns an auto shop."

"Then why has it been there for a week? If he knows someone, it should get done faster, right?"

"Yeah, I suppose. I just thought maybe he was squeezing it in as a favor. And Eric always had a good reason why it wasn't ready yet."

"How convenient. Was his buddy the guy that gave you a tow a few weeks ago?"

Taylor muttered under her breath.

"And overcharged you, right? Did he ever reimburse you?"

"Not yet," Taylor said with a sigh. "And I didn't want to push it. He's helping me out by repairing it in the first place."

A small niggle of worry snaked through her. Mason and his SEAL friends had been furious when they'd found out how much she'd been charged for a tow. She'd been desperate though, and when she'd been stranded on the side of the road, what was she supposed to do? She'd been relieved when her ex had happened to call and sent someone over to help her.

Anchors came into view in the distance. "What time do you need me to pick you up?" Bailey asked.

"I don't get off until one a.m. I'll just grab a ride home with someone. One of the other waitresses should be able to give me a lift."

"You sure?"

"Yeah, sometimes we stay late to wrap up, so I don't want you to have to wait around for me. It shouldn't be a problem to find a ride."

"Have them drop you off at my place," Bailey insisted. "You have a key, so let yourself in. Don't go back to your apartment with Eric there."

"All right," Taylor said, climbing out of her best friend's convertible. "Hopefully he won't wake up until morning. The last thing I need is him coming over to Anchors looking for me."

"Wait—he's done that?" Bailey asked in surprise.

"Just once," Taylor said. "And I told him I was working. He hasn't been back yet, but there's no telling when he'll change his mind."

A couple pushed open the doors to Anchors, and Taylor watched them, thinking the guy in aviators looked like one of Mason's friends. They all kind of blended together sometimes with their buzz cuts, muscles, and bravado—that, and the fact that she usually kept her focus on Mason.

She'd barely noticed the others enough to tell them apart.

The guy in aviators nodded, his gaze locking a moment on Bailey, still seated in the convertible.

"Looks like you've got an admirer," Taylor teased as she shut the passenger door.

"He's with another woman," Bailey said with a laugh, watching them walk down the block toward the ocean. "He's a hottie though. I'd do him."

Taylor nearly choked on her laughter as she stepped away from the car. "You don't even know him."

Bailey shrugged, flashing her a wicked grin. "Be careful tonight, sweetie! Call me if you need anything. Better yet, call that Navy SEAL of yours."

"He's not mine," Taylor protested.

"Uh-huh. Then why's he texting you? And stay away from Eric. The next time he shows up at your apartment—because we both know that he will—do not open the door. Don't even talk to him. Call the police if he won't leave."

"Yeah, maybe I should." She blew out a sigh. She'd been hoping Eric would move on, but that scenario was seeming less and less likely the more he showed up. "Thanks again for the ride, hun."

"Anytime!" Bailey blew her a kiss and then pulled out into traffic, waggling her fingers at the guy in the car behind her who'd let her in.

Bailey was such a flirt. The complete and total opposite of Taylor. They'd been best friends since college though, and Taylor loved her like a sister. Bailey had never met Tessa, but Taylor had a feeling they all would've gotten along amazingly.

Amazing how one small moment had changed her entire life.

Taken Tessa's life.

A brief wave of nervous excitement washed over her as she walked toward Anchors. Although her sister was always in the back of her mind, ten years had let her learn to live with the loss. For the pain to dull slightly. She might miss her terribly sometimes, but she had moved on. Continued living. And without a doubt, she knew Tessa would have wanted that.

She pushed open the door to the popular restaurant and bar. Without thought, her gaze immediately swept to the back where Mason and his buddies usually sat.

It happened to be the area that she usually covered, but since she'd called out, she had no idea which tables would be hers tonight.

A group of military guys was at the back of Anchors, laughing and tossing back beers. Her gaze tracked over them, but then the blond guy at the edge of the table looked up.

Blue eyes immediately locked with hers, and she flushed, looking away. She instantly felt foolish.

Something about Mason always got under her skin.

She didn't even know him that well, but she did know with one hundred percent certainty that he wasn't the type of man Eric was. Mason and his friends loved flirting with women, but they respected them. Treated them right.

He was obviously interested in her, and she kept holding him at an arm's length.

She glanced back again, feeling more confident, and his eyes were still on her.

He grinned in that easy, confident way he always had, his blue eyes sparking with interest. His cropped blond hair gleamed in the overhead lights, and she tried not to stare at his tanned, toned arms. At his impossibly broad chest. The tee shirt he had on stretched across it, revealing his muscles, and he was leaning back in his chair, relaxed and confident as always.

She smiled back, unable to help herself, warmth surging through her chest. Butterflies fluttered in her stomach, and her skin heated.

It was amazing how one look from Mason was all it took to set her ablaze. When those blue eyes locked with hers, she always felt lost to everything but him.

Forget her ex.

She was moving on with her life starting right now.

Chapter 3

Mason laughed, taking another swig of his beer from their table in the back of Anchors. Music blasted from the stereo, loud conversations filled the air around them, and they were all on their second round of beers.

"She was into you, man," Hunter said with a chuckle, watching as a scantily clad woman walked away, pouting.

"Totally," Emma agreed from beside him. "Women don't just throw themselves at men like that unless they think it's a sure thing."

"Kind of like when we met, huh?" Hunter asked, waggling his eyebrows.

Emma flushed as she laughed in embarrassment. "You were hitting on me at the pub! Mason was there. Mason, tell everyone that Hunter is unequivocally making that up."

"I don't know," Camila purred from beside

Colton, brushing her long, dark hair back from her face as she leaned closer to him. "Colton threw himself at me, and I was anything but a sure thing."

The rest of the table howled with laughter as Colton shook his head good naturedly. "It's different with a woman—it's never a sure thing."

"Unless you meet her on the street corner," Hunter quipped.

Colton chuckled. "We met at the airport—and Camila did her damnedest to brush me off without a second glance."

"I had to play hard to get, no?" Camila asked innocently. "Where's the fun in throwing myself at a man?"

"It would've been fun for me," he quipped as the others burst into rowdy laughter once more. Colton was casually leaning back into his chair, his arm securely around Camila. Emma was perched beside Hunter, delicately nibbling on her hamburger. Hunter had already wolfed his down earlier, and he was nabbing fries from her plate.

Ryker was silently scanning the restaurant, and Mason followed his gaze. He hadn't heard back from Taylor after texting her earlier but tried to shrug it off. She was a big girl.

That still didn't explain why she'd apparently missed another shift at Anchors though.

The hair on the back of his neck prickled a moment later, and he abruptly looked up, his gaze sweeping around the restaurant.

"What's up, man?" Colton asked, noticing his sudden change in demeanor.

"I just thought—yep, there she is," he said, nodding at the front of the restaurant where Taylor had suddenly walked in.

He clenched his fists, resisting the urge to rise and go over to her.

Taylor worked here. She was just arriving for her shift like every other waitress who came in. And furthermore—she wasn't his. No matter how badly he wanted to walk over and see her, flirt a little, watch her flush as he teased her, and ask her why she hadn't been around lately, he needed to let her start her shift.

Her cheeks were pink, her dark ponytail swinging back and forth as she immediately looked toward his table. She had on her usual tee-shirt and jeans uniform that the rest of the wait staff at Anchors wore. The snug-fitting shirt did little to conceal her curves though. He noticed the swell of her breasts, her narrow waist and the slight flare of her hips. She flushed slightly as their eyes locked, looking away from him.

Mason frowned.

Had he been reading her wrong?

But no, she glanced over at him again and gave him a smile, her eyes lighting up as he grinned at her. She paused, her eyes locking with his for a moment longer, and then she was talking to her manager, gesturing toward the front door.

Mason's gaze swept over, half expecting someone to walk in after her. A friend? Roommate? Boyfriend?

His jaw tightened.

But no, she wasn't the type to give him her number and lead him on if she had a boyfriend.

Which made it all the more strange that she'd seemed somewhat elusive lately. He suspected she was the type of woman who didn't give out her number very often. Hell. He'd been in here week after week with his buddies before she felt comfortable enough to give him her number.

For such a seemingly small thing, he sensed it was probably a big deal to her.

"I wonder why they said she called out tonight," Colton said as they watched her talking to her manager. Another waitress walked by, giving Taylor a quick hug. Apparently she really hadn't been around much lately.

"Maybe she's been avoiding Mason," Ryker said with a smirk.

"And avoiding her paycheck along with it?" Mason asked, raising his eyebrows. "Doesn't add up. Besides, she could've easily just told me she wasn't interested, and I would've backed off. She knows that. Hell, she could've told any one of you guys that she wanted me to leave her alone. We're in here all the damn time."

Ryker shrugged, his gaze trailing after two women walking by their table. Each had on a cropped top and a short skirt that barely covered their ass. Mile high come-fuck-me heels. Mason would've been all over that type of woman when he was younger, but now?

His gaze was drawn again toward Taylor.

Those tight jeans and snug tee shirt did more for him than those women flaunting their bodies.

Hell.

When had he turned into such an old man, anyway?

"Excuse me," Ryker said, abruptly standing up from the table. "I'm going to go buy those ladies a drink."

"Both of them?" Hunter asked, grinning. Emma had finished eating and was snuggled up against him, and he absentmindedly caressed her shoulder.

"If I'm lucky," Ryker said with a smirk. "Don't wait up for me, fellas."

The table chuckled as he sauntered away.

"He's never going to change, is he?" Emma asked glancing up at Hunter.

"That's a negative, princess," Hunter said.

"Not a chance in hell," Mason agreed. He watched as Emma nonchalantly took Hunter's hand and almost shook his head in disbelief. A couple of months after they'd met her in London, and those two were head over heels.

He never thought he'd see his SEAL team leader anxious to settle down with a woman, but the truth was stranger than fiction sometimes. Emma had moved in with Hunter—flown across an entire ocean to be with him—and they were happily together now. They had the house. The lovey-dovey looks. All they needed was a dog and the two point five kids to be living the American dream.

"Ryker seems rather happy chasing after women, no?" Camila said from her seat beside Colton. "Men like that have no reason to change."

"Somehow you changed this guy," Mason said, nodding toward Colton. "He wasn't going to let us leave Colombia without you."

"Can you blame him?" Camila teased, pretending to pout at her boyfriend. "Look what he'd be missing out on if he'd left me behind."

Mason smirked in amusement, but Colton's jaw tightened. They joked about their relationship now, but Colton and the rest of the Delta team had rescued Camila from a sex-trafficking ring in Bogota. No one wanted to think about what would've happened if they hadn't gotten to her in time.

It killed Colton and the rest of the guys even now knowing there were other women still being held down there. Not to mention all the other women being trafficked world-wide. There wasn't a hell of a lot one SEAL team could do to rescue every single woman in harm's way though. Mason's mind had been occupied enough with Taylor recently, trying to solve that puzzle.

The conversation continued on around him, but Mason's gaze was again drawn to the front of Anchors as Taylor walked out from behind the bar with a pad and pen in one hand.

Her dark ponytail swished back and forth, her hips swayed slightly as she moved, and then Mason was instinctively rising.

Walking over toward her.

Her lips parted in surprise as she saw him approach, but she paused, waiting for him to get to her.

He noticed the rise and fall of her chest, her breasts pressing against her form-fitting tee shirt. Hell, there were plenty of women in here wearing significantly less than that, but Taylor in a snug shirt and tight jeans was sexy as hell. A long silver pendant was around her neck, and he saw she had tiny silver hoops in her ears.

Nothing about her was flashy or attention seeking like the women who were quite obviously trying too hard, but she sure had his attention every time he walked in.

One glance at her always had his heartrate increasing and his libido rising.

"Long time no see," he said in a low voice, loving the flush that spread over her cheeks as she gazed up at him. At six-foot-two, he towered above her petite frame. Something about that made her all the more appealing to him though. He felt protective of her. Attracted to her.

And definitely interested in getting to know her better.

Preferably intimately, but he'd settle for taking things slowly. At the rate they'd been going, it would be another few weeks before she even agreed to go out with him. It had taken long enough just to get her number.

"You disappeared for a while," she said with a small smile. Her chest rose and fell slightly as she spoke, and he realized she was nervous with the way she was clutching her order pad in a death grip.

He wanted to reach out and caress her bare arm. Feel that soft skin beneath his fingertips. Assure her that she had nothing to worry about with him. Not now and not ever.

She was working though.

And they weren't out on a date or at a party getting to know one another. He shouldn't be wanting to reach out and comfort her at all. Not here anyway. Not right now. "That I did," he agreed. "And now I'm back. Nature of the job," he added with a shrug. "They send us out, and we never know when or for how long."

"Yeah, I wondered since I hadn't seen you around…." Her voice trailed off.

"We were sent out on an op," he said in a low voice. "Unfortunately, we don't get much notice, or I would've let you know you wouldn't see me in here for a while."

"Oh."

A hint of amusement trailed through him at her uncertainty. Did she really think he hadn't been interested?

His gaze found hers. "We never know when we'll get called up or how long we'll be gone. Hell, even if we did, I couldn't share the details. But just because I wasn't here didn't mean I wasn't thinking about you."

A smile spread across her face. "Since your friends weren't around either, I thought maybe that you guys must've all had to go somewhere. Either that or you were all avoiding me," she added, a twinkle in her eyes.

She stepped slightly closer to him as a group of young sailors walked by, heading toward the bar, and he inhaled her clean, fresh scent. She inexplicably smelled like the ocean—like sunshine and sand. Maybe a hint of coconut mixed in. Hell, he'd give anything to pull her closer so he could feel her soft curves against him and inhale that intoxicating scent.

One of the guys accidentally jostled her as he made his way past, and Mason let himself steady her, his fingers running over the bare skin of her upper arm.

She flushed at his touch, stepping back only after the guys cleared the area.

Interest and arousal flared within him at the way she reacted to his simple touch.

Hell, he'd love to have her over him. Under him. In every and any way imaginable. He'd love to take her back to his place, strip off her clothes, and slowly explore every curve of her body.

Her waitressing uniform certainly wasn't meant to be sexy—but something about the way her top hugged her breasts and her jeans clung to her like a second skin had him incredibly attracted to her. Not to mention uncomfortably aroused.

Clearly she was fit and in shape. With just the right number of womanly curves to tempt him without even trying.

"Were you having trouble with your car again?" Mason asked, watching as her pink lips parted in surprise. "I asked our waitress earlier if you were working tonight, and she said you had to call out."

"Oh, something came up," Taylor said lightly. "But I don't actually have a car right now. It's uh, getting repaired. Sort of," she added, again looking flustered. "My friend gave me a lift."

"It's in the shop?" Mason asked raising his eyebrows.

Taylor shifted uncomfortably. "I just need to arrange to get it back. Listen, I need to get orders from a few tables. I'm already late for my shift, and it's filling up fast in here tonight. I'll have to catch up with you later, okay?"

Mason nodded, something about her answer not sitting right with him.

Maybe she couldn't afford whatever repairs she needed? Hopefully she wasn't using the same tow-truck driver who'd jerked her around before. He was still pissed as hell she'd been charged $400 just for a tow.

"Do you need a lift home later on?" he asked. "The guys and I will be hanging out here a while, but I can swing by afterward so you don't have to worry about a ride."

"Oh," she said, sounding surprised. "I'll just catch a ride with one of the other waitresses later. I don't want you to have to go through the trouble of coming back."

"It's no trouble," he assured her. "What time do you get off?"

"I don't get off until one a.m.," she said, flushing again slightly. Her brown eyes locked on his. "Is that too late?"

"For you? Not a chance," he said with a chuckle. "And I don't have PT in the morning, so we're good."

"All right. I'll see you later then?"

"Yep," he confirmed. "I'll be back here at oh-one-hundred."

She wrinkled her brow in confusion, looking cute as hell as she did.

"One a.m.," he said, a smile tugging at the corner of his mouth. "Just text me if you need to stay later or something. I'll wait right outside Anchors for you so you don't have to walk anywhere alone in the dark."

"I usually just walk to the garage with everyone else."

He frowned. "There's no need to since I'm here. I'll be outside the front door. It was good to see you, Taylor. I'm glad you made it in tonight. I was worried since I haven't seen you around much."

"Yeah, it was good to see you too," she said. "I'll see you later on. And thanks again for offering me a ride."

He turned to let her pass by him, resisting the urge to lean over and inhale that coconut and sunshine scent. She turned back and flashed him a smile, her dark ponytail swishing back and forth.

Hell.

Driving her home tonight was going to be the death of him.

Mason watched her walk away, his eyes drawn to

her shapely ass. Damn, she was gorgeous. All of her. Briefly, he had a vision of tugging on that ponytail, tilting her head back as he claimed her soft mouth. Letting his fingers trail over her delicate neck as he kissed her.

He'd love to run his hand down that long necklace she had on, letting his hand drift between her breasts.

Pressing his hard body up against all her soft curves.

Kissing her until she was softly moaning against him.

Not that he'd be doing any of that tonight. Taylor was a woman you took things slowly with. The slow burn of the heat between them was intriguing as hell. And judging from the electricity that always sparked between them, he had a feeling she would be worth the wait.

Chapter 4

Taylor eyed the clock on the back wall of Anchors hours later.

12:45 a.m.

She'd been rushing around all night bringing drinks to tables, filling food orders, and collecting tips. Fortunately, the kitchen closed at midnight and last call had been fifteen minutes ago. She swiped a hand across her forehead, tucking her phone into the back pocket of her jeans.

Mason had texted that he was on his way, and she was rethinking letting him give her a lift.

They'd been casually flirting with each other for months, but now that he was giving her a ride, she was positive that he'd ask her out. For real this time—not just teasing her about it in front of the guys. And she wouldn't have been opposed to that aside from Eric.

Ugh.

There was no way he'd be happy about her dating another man. Not that she and Mason were "dating." But one date could lead to another, and she could never invite Mason over. Ever. Not when there was a chance of Eric showing up drunk again.

She shuddered.

Mason could certainly handle himself and wouldn't likely have a problem telling Eric to leave, but what about when he wasn't around?

Eric would be lurking in the shadows, furious. Livid that she'd moved on.

Insisting that she let him in so they could talk. Get back together.

"You okay?" one of the other waitresses, Amy, asked, raising her eyebrows as she watched Taylor.

"Yep. Just tired. It's been a long night."

Amy eyed her, clearly not believing a word. "Thanks, have a good night!" she called out, waving goodbye to a group of regulars. Taylor watched the group of guys leaving, one of them helping their buddy who'd clearly had a few too many.

"Give me your keys, man," his friend ordered. "There's no way in hell you're driving like this."

The guy slumped over, and his friend hauled him to his feet, easily pocketing his keys. The door opened just as they were about to head out, and Taylor was surprised to see Mason coming in. He nodded at her but leaned against the wall by the door, clearly intending to wait until she finished her shift and was ready to go.

The question was, should she head over to Bailey's apartment like they'd discussed?

Or dare try her own?

Eric might still be passed out drunk on her sofa,

but what if he'd woken up after a few hours? She wanted him out of there, not crashing at her place. She bit her lip, still undecided. He probably would've texted her to complain if he woke up and she was gone.

To her best friend's house it was.

"That your ride?" Amy asked, nodding toward Mason. "He was in here earlier with his friends, right?"

"Yeah, that's Mason. He's stationed over at Little Creek, so he and his friends are in here a lot. You'll start to recognize them, I'm sure. We always have a bunch of regulars that hang out here—men and women alike."

"Are you guys dating?" Amy asked, clearing the empty plates and glasses from the table beside her. She pocketed the tip, looking relieved.

Taylor could relate. Most of the regular customers tipped well, but every once in a while, they'd be working the same table for hours and barely have anything to show for it.

"No, we're not dating, but he offered to drive me home when he found out that I still don't have my car. He's asked me out—sort of. I'm just…taking my time…."

Her voice trailed off, and Mason waved as the two women looked over at him. Taylor blushed furiously, knowing that he'd realize they were talking about him.

Good grief.

She was a grown, twenty-seven-year-old woman. Why was she acting like a school girl with a crush on the captain of the football team?

He'd offered her a ride. He had her cell number. It wasn't exactly a secret that she was interested in him.

Or vice versa.

Something about Mason always made her stomach do flips though.

He was almost boyishly good looking, aside from the muscles on top of muscles that were clearly the result of his training as a Navy SEAL. His broad shoulders and muscled chest gave way to a trim waistline. His jeans hung slightly from his hips, leading down straight toward the promised land. With his height, she had no doubt he had an impressive package.

Not that she planned to be getting up close and personal with that anytime soon.

She hurried, fumbling with the empty beer bottles she'd picked up in her haste. They clinked together, drawing the attention of the other wait staff cleaning up. The last few patrons began to exit Anchors, leaving mostly empty tables aside from a few stragglers at the bar.

"Hun, a guy like him could have anyone he wants," Amy said. "Don't take too much time," she added with a wink.

"Yeah. I hear ya," Taylor said, carrying her heavy tray stacked high with empty plates and beer bottles back toward the kitchen.

Finally, twenty minutes later, she was exiting the back of Anchors and walking toward Mason's grinning face. "Sorry, I'm running late," she said. "Closing always takes longer than expected. Some of the others on the kitchen staff will be here another hour doing clean up."

"It's no problem. I offered you a lift, so I don't mind the wait."

He held open the door, and then his large frame

was following her outside. A cool breeze blew in from the ocean, and she shivered slightly, running her hands over her bare arms. Her body electrified as Mason came to a stop beside her, and she could feel the heat radiating off his large, muscular frame.

She glanced up at him, her own head barely coming up to his shoulder. He towered over her, but she felt safe. Protected. When was the last time she'd come out of work at this hour and not looked around? Not watched for someone to jump out of the shadows?

Never, she thought wryly.

Although she always made sure to walk to the parking garage with the others, it felt good having Mason here beside her. Safe.

"Wow, look at that full moon tonight," she said, pausing for a moment in awe as she glanced up at the sky. She was at the beach nearly every day, but something about the moonlight reflecting off the dark ocean water was captivating. She wished she had her camera with her. The scene before them would be an amazing photograph.

"It's gorgeous," Mason agreed, his voice husky. "Come on," he said, taking her hand in his warm, muscular one. "Let's go check it out for a few minutes before I drive you home."

His thick fingers wove between hers, and heat surged through her as he guided her along. He confidently strode down toward the water, a mass of muscle and movement. This was a man used to running for miles, jumping out of airplanes, swimming in dark waters.

What must he think of her?

If he knew she was afraid to even leave her own

apartment because of her ex, he'd probably be mystified. This was the type of man afraid of nothing.

"It's cold out here," she said, shivering slightly as they walked closer to the ocean.

Mason chuckled, tucking her under his arm and pulling her close. The weight of his arm wrapped around her shoulders made her imagine what it would be like to feel the weight of his muscular body moving over her. Making love to her.

He smelled clean, with just the faintest hint of spice. And he was all rippling muscles under that tanned, toned flesh. Pure male.

"Hell, sweetheart, I've free dived in freezing cold ocean water in the middle of winter. This feels pretty damn temperate in comparison."

Taylor giggled, loving the feeling of Mason's warm, solid body pressed against hers. They paused at the railing of the boardwalk, taking in the stretch of sand and dark water before them. Warm lamplight dotted the boardwalk all the way up and down the tourist strip of the beach for endless blocks, but the ocean in front of them was dark aside from the glow of the moonlight.

Waves crashed on the shore, lulling her into a sense of contentment, and then Mason was easing her in front of him, wrapping his arms completely around her. She relaxed against him, his broad chest pressed against her back. Her heart pounded at his closeness, her breath catching as he rested his chin atop her head.

She felt like they were a couple in that brief moment—Mason holding her in his arms. Keeping her warm. Shielding her from the world.

She always felt safe when he was around.

Fortunately, Eric had never come into Anchors looking for her when Mason was here, but Taylor had a feeling that if he had, Mason and his friends would've set him straight.

And there was a certain sense of security in that.

If only she could get him to quit showing up at her apartment.

Mason's arms tightened ever-so-slightly around her, bringing her mind back to the present. Wouldn't she love to go out with Mason sometime, bring him back to her apartment, and explore that spectacular body of his. Let him kiss and caress her as they made out on her sofa. Get lost in those gorgeous blue eyes of his.

He always teased her at Anchors, casual and flirty, but she could sense the serious side of him as well.

He was committed to his job—to his career in the Navy. To life as a SEAL. Sure, he had fun with his buddies, but they were out risking their lives. Saving lives.

It was a lot different than her ex, who couldn't even hold down a job for more than a month at a time.

She let out a wistful sigh.

"I wish it wasn't so late," Mason said, his lips moving against her hair.

"I know. Normally I don't mind working these hours at Anchors, but I wish you and I were here earlier," she said with a yawn. "I'm past the days where I want to stay up on the beach until dawn."

She felt his smile against her head. "Me too. But we'll come down here another evening. We'll go to dinner, go walk down the boardwalk, the whole deal."

"That'd be nice," she agreed. "As long as we don't

eat at Anchors."

Mason chuckled, his lips brushing against her hair. "But I love that place."

"You'll just have to make do eating somewhere else, I suppose," she teased.

"I can live with that," he agreed. "It's almost one-thirty in the morning; I should get you home."

"Yeah, probably," she agreed. "I do need my beauty sleep."

"I should've brought you a sweatshirt or something," he said as she shivered again in the night air. "I keep extra PT gear in the back of my SUV."

"I'm fine," she insisted. He took her hand as they walked back toward Anchors. She flushed as his thumb lightly grazed over her skin, but a beat later he was already releasing it and pulling open the door to his SUV. Mason helped her climb inside, and then he was shutting the door and rounding the car. Pulling open the driver's side door and climbing in.

"You live over by the north end of the beach, right?"

"Yeah, but I'm staying at my best friend's tonight. Other direction."

Mason nodded but didn't ask any questions as he started the engine. He expertly maneuvered his SUV out of the spot on the street and pulled onto Atlantic Avenue, nearly empty at this time of night.

It felt strangely intimate driving alone with him in the dark. How many times had she waited on their table over the past few months? Twenty? Thirty? Mason always had a grin on his face and a gleam in his eye when he looked at her, but this one-on-one attention had her heart rate accelerating and nervous butterflies fluttering in her stomach.

And all she was doing was sitting beside him.

Goodness. She'd fall head over heels if she wasn't careful. And she'd just gotten out of a relationship. Even though she knew Mason was nothing like her ex, she still needed to tread carefully. Out of the frying pan and into the fire and all that. She didn't sense Mason would ever be a bigger problem than Eric, but what did she know?

She certainly hadn't been a very good judge of character before.

Three years with her ex, and she hadn't even been able to move on because he was still darkening her doorstep.

"Thanks for letting me give you a lift," Mason said, his voice deep.

Taylor laughed and glanced over at him. "I should be thanking you for the ride, not the other way around."

He chuckled. "Well, I have to admit I was hoping you'll let me take you out one night. I didn't want to scare you off by asking you out in front of everyone at Anchors tonight. You already shot me down once in front of the guys, but since you gave me your number and haven't told me to stop texting, I'm hoping you'll let me take you on an actual date. I promise to leave the rest of my SEAL team at home." He glanced over at her, and although she couldn't see his expression in the shadows, she sensed he was smiling.

"I'd like that," she said.

"Fantastic. And aside from my wanting to take you out, my buddies have been giving me hell ever since you turned me down in front of them."

"Oh, I didn't mean—"

"I'm just teasing you, sweetheart," he said with a low chuckle. "I can handle my SEAL team. Hell, we rib each other all the time. Fight like brothers, sometimes."

"You guys do seem really close."

"Yep," he confirmed. "We train together, work together, fight together—know what each of the other guys is thinking. We have to in our line of work. Lives are at stake—literally."

"It sounds dangerous," she said.

He nodded. "It can be, just like any other job in the military. But that's why we train hard and drill together. We have to be prepared for anything. And like I mentioned before—sometimes we do have to up and leave at a moment's notice. We have hours to be wheels up. So, if you don't see us around, or you haven't heard from me for some reason, it's not because I'm avoiding you."

"I understand," she said softly.

"You haven't been around Anchors much either though lately. I haven't seen you there since we got back from our last op aside from tonight. I have to ask, is everything all right?"

"Yeah, everything's fine. It's just…complicated."

She turned to look at him as they pulled to a stop at a red light, taking in his strong profile. His eyes briefly met hers in the dim light.

"I know we don't know each other well," he said, his voice gruff. "Hell, I'd like to get to know you better. I think you know that. But if you're having trouble of some sort, you can tell me about it. Whatever it is, I'll do my best to help you."

He glanced over at her again as he pulled forward, and she sighed. "It's just kind of a weird situation," she admitted. "I didn't really want to drag you into it."

"Try me," he said easily. "Can I go with you to pick up your car? If it's a money issue or something, I can talk to them. You paid way too much for that tow a few weeks ago. If anything, they can take that off the cost of the repairs."

"No, no, it's not money," she said flushing as waves of embarrassment washed over her. At least it was dark inside Mason's SUV. He was a Navy SEAL for goodness sake. He probably got hazard duty or some kind of bonus every time he was sent out on a mission. She was just a waitress—granted, she loved her job and the freedom the evening shift gave her. She had free time to pursue her passions like photography and just enjoy life by the beach. It wouldn't be the first time someone thought she couldn't afford something though.

"So, there's a problem with your apartment?" he hedged. "You're staying with a friend…."

"It's my ex," she said, nervously wringing her hands together. "He's at my apartment right now."

"He lives with you?" Mason asked, his voice tight.

A beat passed.

"No, no, nothing like that. We broke up a month ago, but he keeps showing up. He came over earlier, completely wasted, and wanted to crash there. I called out from work at first because I didn't think I should leave."

"What do you mean?" Mason asked. His voice sounded dark. Dangerous. She was used to him flirting with her, but this was a new side of him. Suddenly he was all business, and he didn't sound happy about what she'd said.

"He showed up drunk earlier. It's not the first time," she admitted. "I just—"

"Does he have a key?"

"No, and if he did, I'd change the locks. I don't want him around at all, actually, but he's been coming over more and more. I just didn't want to make him angry and refuse to let him inside."

Mason didn't say anything, and Taylor glanced over in his direction. She couldn't fully see his profile in the moonlight, but his jaw was clenched, his fists gripping the steering wheel. He took a deep breath, and for a beat, she worried that maybe she shouldn't have told him.

That he was mad at her.

"Are you…upset?"

"At you? Hell no. Taylor, sweetheart, if he shows up when you don't want him around, you do not have to let him in. You broke up, and he needs to accept that. No matter what he says or what he tells you, you have the right to tell him no. Call me next time, and I'll be there immediately. I don't care what I'm doing, who I'm with—I'll drop it and come."

Taylor blinked, slightly flustered as a feeling of warmth spread through her. Mason wasn't angry at her, he was angry on her behalf. Because of her asshole ex.

Just like her best friend had been.

She had to admit that Mason was a lot more intimidating than Bailey though. If Bailey had mouthed off to Eric, he'd probably just laugh in his drunken stupor and push past her.

But Mason?

She didn't doubt that he could handle Eric. The trouble was, Mason was gone a lot of the time. She helplessly shrugged. "I don't know when he'll come, and you're not always around. Not that you have to be," she hastily added, "I just mean sometimes you guys disappear for a while, so I figure you're out of the country or something…."

Her voice trailed off. Mason hadn't explicitly told her what they did when he left, but she could put two and two together just like anyone else. He didn't just disappear—his entire team did. And then a few days or few weeks later, they'd be back as if nothing had happened.

He didn't have to say that they were traveling overseas on missions for her to figure that one out.

He blew out a frustrated sigh.

"True, but I have plenty of friends on base. Guys on another SEAL team even. I'll get you the number of Ice, their SEAL team leader. If you can't get a hold of me, I want you to call him."

"Ice?"

"It's his nickname. Patrick 'Ice' Foster. He's a good guy—you'd like him. Married with a couple of kids."

"I can't drag them into this."

"Hopefully you won't have to. But we all look out for one another. Hell, his own wife—girlfriend at the time—was stalked by someone a couple of years ago. All the guys on the Alpha SEAL team watched out for her. The next time your ex comes around, call me. I'm not expecting him to keep coming back after we're through."

"I don't want to get you into some sort of trouble. Oh, take the next right. My best friend lives in the apartments off Juniper."

"Gotcha," he said, his voice tight.

Mason followed her directions, pulling into the apartment complex. He shut off the engine and glanced over at her, his face tense in the street lights from the lot. "I'll help you figure this out, sweetheart. Hell, whether you want to go out with me or not, I'll help you. No man should be forcing a woman to let him into her apartment, uninvited, and I want this taken care of before the situation escalates. Before I have to leave again and you're here all alone."

She nodded, heat coursing through her. Having a man like Mason concerned about her was intimidating in an entirely different way. He was concerned about her. Could protect her. But what about when he was gone? Or got bored and moved on?

She couldn't let herself fall for a man like him, despite how much she appreciated him being here now. Despite how badly she wanted to be with him.

She was attracted to him and intrigued by him, but then what?

He'd move on, maybe even bring a date into Anchors, and she'd be on the outside looking in. Watching him and his buddies have a good time while she pretended that it didn't hurt.

"How long did you say you were together?" Mason asked when she hadn't said anything.

"Three years. He was shocked when I broke up with him, and I—I don't like that he's been coming around more and more. Instead of moving on and getting past our breakup, he seems like he's trying to get back together with me. He keeps showing up, insisting that we talk and he come in. Of course, he's too drunk to have much of a conversation about anything."

"Does he know where your friend lives?" Mason

asked, nodding toward the building.

"Bailey? Yeah, of course. We dated for several years, so he's been here plenty of times. He wasn't always an asshole," she added. "Things started to sour when he began drinking more. He couldn't hold down a steady job, and the guys he hangs around with are bad news."

Mason nodded, seemingly lost in thought. "All right. I'll walk you to the door," he said, climbing out of the vehicle.

Taylor was already climbing out of the SUV by the time he rounded the front.

"I would've helped you," he said, his voice deep.

She grabbed her purse from the front seat, stepping back as Mason shut the door. "I'm fine."

"Maybe I just wanted an excuse to hold you close," he said, his voice gruff.

His arm draped over her shoulders, and he pulled her toward him like they belonged together. Like they were a couple heading home for the evening, not a man dropping off a waitress he barely even knew.

Okay, so she was slightly more than just his waitress.

He'd gotten her number, they'd texted, he'd asked her out.

That didn't mean she should make any more out of this than what it was though.

He frowned as they walked toward the apartment building. "I don't like that you work such late hours—it's not safe for a single woman to be out alone this late at night. Especially not with a jilted ex following you around."

"I've had this shift for months—you guys should know. You're in Anchors all the time."

"Yep," he agreed with a chuckle. "Guilty as charged. And hell if I didn't like seeing you there." His hand rested on the small of her back as they walked up the stairs of the garden style apartment building, the heat from his skin blazing through the tee shirt she had on. It felt like he was leaving an imprint on her skin—branding her with his mark.

And she liked his touch a little too much.

Maybe they'd go out a few times, but men like him didn't usually settle down. They were gone too much for a serious relationship.

And she had a feeling that if she fell for him, she'd fall hard. Too hard.

Maybe he wasn't like Eric, but he was dangerous in his own way.

A dog barked in the parking lot, drawing her attention from the open stairwell, but aside from the lone man walking his dog, no one else was around. She felt safe with Mason at her side. Protected. And despite the chill in the air, warmth radiated off him.

His large frame hovered behind hers, shielding her from the rest of the world.

Mason wouldn't always be around though. She needed to handle her situation herself. Or at least try to.

They paused at Bailey's front door, Mason's hand hovering on her waist as he towered over her.

"I'd love to kiss you goodnight, but I'll save that for our first actual date."

She flushed, and he chuckled again. Her eyes were drawn to his full lips, and his fingers lightly trailed over her cheek. "I love how you blush around me."

"It's embarrassing," she protested.

"It's attractive as hell. And I love that I can get

that kind of reaction from you. It makes me wonder how you'd react when we're really alone sometime." He paused, the air thick with tension, and Taylor wondered if he was going to kiss her anyway, despite what he said.

He dropped his hand to his side, and she tried not to feel disappointed at the loss of his touch. His blue gaze met hers.

"I know you work nights at Anchors," Mason said. "When's a good time to take you out on an actual date? I loved driving you home, but that doesn't count. I figure you probably can't get the night off tomorrow on such short notice."

"Saturday's our busiest night," she agreed. "I can't call out now, especially since I've missed a couple of shifts lately."

Mason nodded, waiting for her to continue.

"I'm off Sunday though if you're free then."

"Perfect. I know we said dinner, but it's supposed to be great weather this weekend. How about we plan for something Sunday afternoon instead?"

"What'd you have in mind?"

"It's a surprise," he said, his lips quirking into a smile.

"Well you have to give me some hint. What am I supposed to bring or wear?"

"Fair enough," he said easily. "Let's plan on lunch outdoors. That's all the details I'm going to tell you for now."

"Fair enough? That's not fair at all," she pouted.

He grinned, his blue eyes sparking. "Goodnight Taylor. Next time I'm dropping you off at your place, and I definitely plan on kissing you goodnight."

She flushed again, imagining those full lips moving

over hers. Would he kiss her lightly? Pull her to him? Pin her against the door and kiss her senseless?

"Text me your address tomorrow. I'll let you know what time I'll be by on Sunday to pick you up."

"Until Sunday," she said.

He brushed a lock of hair that had slipped free from her ponytail back from her face, his fingers leaving a trail of heat over her skin in their wake.

"Until Sunday," he repeated. "I'm looking forward to it. Goodnight Taylor."

He took a step back, watching as she produced a key from her purse and unlocked the door to Bailey's apartment. When she glanced back a moment later, he was gone.

Chapter 5

"Hoorah!" Jacob shouted the next afternoon, leaping off the edge of the dock and into the Atlantic Ocean. He disappeared underwater for a moment, sunlight glistening off the blue water, and Mason smirked as the women around them gasped.

"Is he going to be okay?" a brunette with freckles asked, looking worried. "The water is so deep way out here!"

Noah adjusted his aviators and grinned, his gaze raking over her slender body, clad in a bright yellow bikini. "Angel, we're in the Navy. It's pretty much a requirement we know how to swim."

"Will you rescue me if I fall in?" she asked, taking a step closer toward him. She trailed her bright red fingernails up his forearm, and Mason could swear she was batting her eyelashes beneath those oversized sunglasses she wore.

He resisted the urge to groan.

"Are you guys based out of Little Creek?" the blonde asked Mason, unabashedly adjusting her skimpy string bikini top. Her breasts were barely contained by the small scraps of fabric, but they looked fake from a mile away. Jacob hadn't seemed to mind though.

"Guilty as charged," Mason said, his gaze shifting back to the water.

Jacob emerged a moment later, grinning as the women watched him. He gripped the edge of the wooden dock with two hands and effortlessly hefted himself out of the water, his dripping wet body standing before them.

"Yay!" the blonde clapped, rushing over to give him a hug.

"Now that's the kind of greeting I like," Jacob said. "It's not the same swimming with my Navy buddies."

Mason turned away as the two women fawned over his friends. He'd met up with Jacob and Noah intending to spend some time on the beach tossing a football around and admiring the bikini-clad locals.

The guys seemed more interested in the college students who'd come over and started flirting with them though. Their football and towels lay abandoned back on the beach. Mason's gaze drifted over the people milling about on the sand. A couple walked by, hand-in-hand, young families chased after their kids. A group of young military guys lay stretched out on towels close to the water.

His mind drifted back to Taylor and last night. To holding her against him as they'd briefly gazed out at the moonlit water. Her body had melded perfectly to his like she'd belonged there.

Hell.

When had he gotten so damn sappy?

He was attracted to her. So what of it? She was a beautiful woman.

He'd resisted the urge to text her this morning, knowing she was at her friend's place. Now that several hours had gone by and he hadn't heard from her though, he couldn't stop himself from making sure she was okay.

He figured her ex would leave when he realized she wasn't there, but what did he know? It couldn't hurt to make sure the asshole was long gone.

He grabbed his phone from the pocket of his swim trunks and thumbed a quick text.

Did you make it home okay?

Shrieks of laughter erupted behind him, and he saw Noah swinging the brunette in his arms, pretending he was going to toss her into the ocean.

His phone buzzed with a text, and he saw Taylor's immediate response.

Yes, Bailey drove me back. My ex was gone. Thank God!

He frowned. She shouldn't need to worry about going back to her own apartment. She'd assured him she wouldn't be alone since her best friend was giving her a lift, but a part of him had wanted to see her safely home.

To check out for himself that the man who'd barged in to her place was long gone.

Hell.

She wasn't his. They hadn't even been out on an actual date. Her smile, coconut scent, and tempting curves were damn near impossible to get out of his head though.

I'm at the beach with the guys. I much preferred your

company last night though.

He imagined Taylor blushing as she read his text. She embarrassed easily, no matter how innocent his flirtations were.

She had such a smooth, porcelain complexion. He wondered if that flush across her cheeks would spread over the rest of her fair skin. He was dying to see what it would look like when she came, her body flushed and sated, her breasts swollen, her sex slickened with arousal.

Her curves up against his muscular frame would be fucking spectacular.

And hell if he wouldn't love to explore every one of them.

He would love to run his hands and lips all over her delectable body.

To kiss her and tease her for hours—and then finally claim her as his.

His phone buzzed, drawing him out of his daydream. *I'm looking forward to seeing you tomorrow.*

He quickly thumbed a response.

Me too, sweetheart. Stay safe until then.

Worry niggled at the back of his mind. As far as he knew, she still didn't have her car. He couldn't keep chauffeuring her around. It's not like she was his girlfriend or something. And damn. When was the last time he'd even had a serious relationship?

Dating a woman for a few weeks and then moving on had served him well in the past. What was so different about this woman that had his head spinning in circles, his cock hardening every time she was near, and his protective instincts soaring?

He frowned as he heard a shriek and a splash, and saw that Noah had actually jumped in the water with the woman.

She clung to him as they emerged from the ocean a moment later, and Jacob bent down from the deck to help haul her up.

Mason raised his eyebrows as Noah climbed back onto the deck again. He shrugged easily, grabbing his aviators from where he'd set them down. "She dared me to do it," he said with a chuckle.

"Oh, you are in so much trouble," she said, playfully pouting at him.

"We're going to go grab drinks and apps at one of the bars," Jacob said, nodding toward the string of oceanfront hotels and restaurants along the boardwalk. "Want to come with?"

"Nah, another time," Mason said. "I'll catch up with you guys later."

He turned, walking alone down the dock back toward the sand. Normally he'd be all about having beers with his buddies and a couple of women, but those two college-aged girls were just that—girls. Silly. Predictable. A sure thing.

He had Taylor had been dancing around their flirtation for months.

And something about the slow burn between them would make the victory all that much sweeter.

Chapter 6

Taylor blew out a sigh as Amy pulled to a stop in front of Taylor's apartment building. The clock on the car's dashboard read 11:17. It had been another busy night at Anchors, with running orders for table after table all night. Normally she didn't mind the weekend rush, but a part of her had hoped that Mason would show up during her shift.

Which was silly.

He and his Navy friends had just been there the night before. She usually saw him when she saw him, and that was that. They already had plans for the next day. He'd sent her a string of texts that afternoon. Yet her stomach had fluttered every time the door had opened, and she'd secretly hoped he'd come walking in.

"When's your car supposed to be ready?" Amy asked, unlocking the doors. "It seems like they're scamming you holding it for so long."

"Soon. Supposedly. And I know—the shop is owned by my ex's friend. I'm pretty sure he's giving me the run around just to be a jackass."

"You should send those guys you know over to pick it up for you. The Navy SEALs? One look from them, and they'll be handing over your keys."

"Yeah, Mason actually offered to go with me. If I don't get it back soon, I might have to take him up on it. I can't keep having everyone drive me around. Thanks again for the lift," she said, opening the passenger door.

"Are you off tomorrow?" Amy asked.

Taylor smiled as she peeked back into the door. "Yep. Mason and I are going out."

"Wait—we've been working together all day, and you are just now mentioning that?" Amy shrieked.

"Like you said, we were working. I didn't get a chance."

"Uh-uh. Well I'm working all day tomorrow, so have fun, sister. He's a hottie. I want to hear all the details next time."

"You bet. Thanks again," she said, closing the passenger door. Heat flushed across her cheeks, despite the coolness in the night air. Goodness. Every single time she even thought of Mason, her entire body alighted with warmth.

It had been that way for months—waiting their table had been excruciating at first. She'd been sure she'd drop the entire tray of drinks with the way her hands shook or trip right in front of him and make a fool of herself.

Not that they gave her a hard time—a couple of the other guys had ribbed Mason about her a bit. And she'd certainly known that he was interested in her.

But every time those blue eyes met hers, she'd felt like he could see right through her. It was as if he could look past her hesitancy around him, her nervousness, and see straight into her very soul.

Amy's car pulled away, and Taylor crossed the parking lot toward her apartment building, gazing up at the faint stars in the sky. Adrenaline pumped through her, and she had the crazy urge to go down to the beach. She'd love to walk along the sand in the darkness, listening to the waves crashing on the shore. Clearing her head. Letting the cool breeze wash over her.

Not that she'd feel comfortable venturing there alone at this time of night. Although it was a relatively safe area, walking around alone in the dark wasn't necessarily a smart move. Ever.

The boardwalk was relatively safe with all the hotels and restaurants that ran along it, but the quieter north end of the beach where she lived was secluded at this time of night.

She squinted up at the stars again, but the lamplights in the parking lot and light coming from the apartments kept her from really seeing them well.

She walked into her apartment building, similar to the walk-up garden style one her best friend Bailey lived in. She lightly climbed the open staircase, not wanting to wake her neighbors.

The sound of a TV came from behind one door, and laughter erupted behind another, but she knew some families had young kids and babies that were fast asleep.

When she reached the third floor, she turned toward her own apartment as she dug her keys from her purse and gasped.

Eric lay slouched over, passed out on her doormat, a smooshed bouquet of flowers next to him. His chest rose and fell slightly, and she took in his rumpled appearance. His tee shirt was slightly pulled out from his jeans, an empty beer can lay crushed next to him, dark circles were under his eyes, and he looked like he hadn't shaved in several days.

She hedged slightly closer, and heard his quiet snore.

Shit.

If she opened the door to her apartment, he'd fall into her foyer.

What was she supposed to do? Drag his large body out of the way?

She looked at the other doors in the hallway, as if that would somehow give her an answer. Maybe if someone came out they could help her move him?

But then what if he woke up?

Blowing out a sigh, she took her cell phone from her purse. There were no texts from him, so clearly he'd intended to surprise her.

And he must have known she'd be home late at night after her shift at Anchors.

Alone.

She'd been pleasantly surprised to find him gone this morning—her front door had been locked, there was no note. She was guessing he'd woken up and not even remembered what had happened.

So why the hell was he here again now?

She turned back to the stairs, quietly walking back down the way she'd just come. The rubber sole of her sneaker squeaked on the metal tread, and she froze.

Hell.

She glanced up the empty stairwell but didn't see

anyone. Didn't hear any movement.

That didn't mean she wanted to stick around and wait for him to wake up though. She huffed out a frustrated sigh. She couldn't even get in her car and drive over to Bailey's apartment since she didn't have it. Thanks to Eric.

So much for taking a long, hot shower and crashing in her own bed. She'd already spent last night at Bailey's and was looking forward to relaxing at home tonight.

This entire situation was getting ridiculous.

She quickly texted her best friend. Bailey's reply came back a moment later.

Bryan is over here, but we can come get you.

Shoot.

If her best friend was on a date, she didn't want to go crash over there. Or have her drive all the way across town to get her. Maybe she should just call a cab? Stay at a hotel?

Don't worry, I'll figure something else out.
Enjoy the night with your new man.

Scrolling through the contact list on her phone, Taylor hovered over Mason's name. He'd said to call him if Eric showed up, but not even twenty-four hours had gone by. She couldn't just expect him to come running every time her ex was around. And it's not like Mason could even tell him to buzz off since Eric was currently passed out drunk.

Again.

What was he going to do? Wait around all night for him to wake up so they could talk man to man? Give her a ride to a hotel?

Blowing out a sigh, she decided to text him anyway. If they had plans for tomorrow, she had to at least let him know she might not be at her own place tonight.

And that her ex might be around tomorrow when Mason came to pick her up.

Goodness.

Why did she always feel like such a hot mess around Mason anyway? First her car trouble, then her ex. He was going to lose interest before they ever even had a date at this rate.

Quickly typing a message before she lost her nerve, she sent him a text.

Are you up?

Mason's reply buzzed almost instantly.

Getting ready for bed. Did you just home from work?
I'm looking forward to our date tomorrow.

Heat flooded her cheeks, but she tried to tame her excitement. She needed to figure out where to go for the night. How to handle Eric. She'd worry about her date with Mason tomorrow.

She quickly thumbed a response.

I'm in the parking lot of my apartment. Eric is passed out on my doorstep.

My ex.

Mason didn't reply immediately, and a brief feeling of doubt washed over her. Maybe she shouldn't have texted him? He could be tired and not want her bothering him this late at night. It wasn't like this was an emergency or something.

It wasn't like Mason was her boyfriend.

She probably should've just gotten a cab ride to a hotel and checked in for the night. She didn't have any of her things but—

Mason's name flashed across the screen of her cell phone with an incoming call.

"Hello?" she squeaked.

"I'm on my way over," he said, his voice deep. Authoritative. Inexplicably, a feeling of calm washed over her. "If he's not up when I get there, I'll drag him out of the way so you can get inside. We'll put him in a cab and send him on his way. I'm headed north on Atlantic Avenue, so text me your address."

"Wait—what? You're driving over here now?"

"Already on my way."

"I thought you were getting ready for bed."

Her eyes drifted across the lot as she spotted a couple walking hand-in-hand toward a convertible. It had been so long since she'd been in a happy relationship, the image almost looked foreign to her.

Like something out of a fairy tale.

"I was, but now I'm on my way to get you. If your ex is passed out drunk, I can't exactly have a talk with him now. But I don't want to leave you there alone. I can move him out of the way so you can get into your place, but I don't want him to wake up and pound on your door in a couple of hours. Not with you there alone.

"But—"

"I assume you still don't have your car?"

"No, not yet."

"I can drive you back to my place. Or your friend's," he quickly added. "Wherever you'd be comfortable. Or I can stay at your place tonight and tell him to get lost in case he comes back pounding on your door."

"I don't know," she said nervously. "I don't want him to get mad. If he wants to talk and you're there…."

Her voice trailed off, and she hated how weak she

sounded. How she was letting Eric manipulate the situation even now after they'd broken up.

"Sweetheart, he needs to get over it. To move on. Maybe he can't take no for an answer from you, but if I open your front door, believe me, he won't be coming back."

"Okay. I'm just worried."

"There's nothing to worry about," Mason assured her. "I can crash on your couch tonight. But don't worry, I know we're just getting to know each other. I don't expect anything from you if I stay the night."

"And tomorrow?"

"What about tomorrow?" he asked.

"Do you still want to go out?"

"Hell yes," he said immediately. "This doesn't change things. I told you last night to call me if your ex showed up, and I'm glad you did. I don't want you to have to worry about him. Hell, like I said, even if you didn't want to go out with me, I'd help you. I don't appreciate a man refusing to leave a woman alone. Continually showing up uninvited. The fact that he keeps coming by when you've told him it's over isn't cool."

"Okay," she said, feeling a little breathless. Mason sounded so angry on her behalf. And he had a right to be, she supposed. He was concerned for her. Maybe they weren't together exactly but they'd known each other for a while. "So, I'll see you soon?"

"Affirmative. I should be there in ten minutes. Stay out front since it's late. Unless he wakes up before I get there—then get somewhere that he can't see you."

"I doubt he'll be up anytime soon. His drinking has gotten worse and worse. Once he passes out, he's out for a couple of hours at least."

"All right, sweetheart. Don't worry. I'm on my way."

Chapter 7

Mason clutched the steering wheel of his SUV, clenching his jaw. He scrubbed a hand over his day-old stubble, frowning. He'd been surprised to hear from Taylor tonight but pleased she'd texted him—until he saw her second text.

His blood boiled at the thought of her asshole ex right outside her front door.

What if he'd been awake when Taylor got home?

Would he have forced himself into her apartment? Forced himself on her?

Guys didn't just keep showing up like that when they were thinking rationally. Hell, he was used to dating women for a few weeks and then moving on. Never giving them another thought.

The fact that Taylor's ex kept showing up more and more unnerved him.

Maybe he hoped to win her back, but the likelihood was that he kept coming around because he wouldn't take no for an answer. He was fixated on her. Obsessed. Maybe he hadn't been until she'd broken up with him, but some guys always wanted what they couldn't have.

Hell.

His phone buzzed with a new text as he drove down Atlantic Avenue, and he saw her address flash across his screen. He was supposed to be picking her up tomorrow afternoon for a date, not rushing over because her asshole of an ex wouldn't leave her alone.

A certain sense of male pride filled his chest though at the fact that she'd texted him for help.

She trusted him to be there for her, relied on him for her safety.

Maybe they hadn't exactly gotten off to a normal start, but hell if he wouldn't do everything in his power to protect her. He wanted to woo her, sure. Take her out, kiss her goodnight, take her to bed.

Eventually.

None of that would ever happen if this was hanging over her shoulders.

Grumbling under his breath, he pulled into the parking lot of Taylor's apartment complex, his gaze sweeping the area. One street light was out in the back corner, but he was pleased to see that it was mostly well lit. The walkways and grounds were well-maintained, with lamp posts scattered throughout. It was relatively safe for a single woman living alone.

Relatively.

Because the breezy, open apartment buildings had no way from keeping Taylor's ex from showing up at her door.

A secure building with a doorman would've been ideal, but that wasn't exactly common in this beach community. People were casual around here. Tourists came and went in the warmer months. They wouldn't want to show identification in gated communities or buildings with security and doormen.

They just wanted to relax and enjoy their vacation.

He quickly shut off the engine and stepped out of his vehicle. He'd been in such a rush, he hadn't even grabbed anything to spend the night here.

A tee shirt and shorts would have to suffice. He could always sleep in his boxers, but he got the impression Taylor wouldn't appreciate that just yet.

Briefly, he wondered what she slept in as he moved across the lot. A sexy little nightie? Comfortable cotton pajamas? Nothing at all?

Not that he'd be finding out tonight.

Her safety was his primary concern, and if she wasn't comfortable with him yet, he'd give her space.

For now.

Taylor was standing by the well-lit stairwell, and he was both relieved and unnerved. She shouldn't be standing around alone this late at night, but she didn't have her car. Couldn't get into her own damn apartment.

Hell.

Her ex was controlling her life whether she realized it or not.

And Mason didn't like it one bit.

Taylor flushed in surprise as she turned and saw him, a relieved smile flashing across her face. "You came."

He ducked down, brushing his lips across her forehead and inhaling her scent of coconut and sunshine. "Of course I came. Did you really think I wouldn't?"

"Yes. I mean no, I mean—" She trailed off, looking flustered. He took her slender hand in his, wanting her close. Needing to see for himself that she was all right.

"I don't like that he's showing up at your apartment late at night," he said, his thumb briefly rubbing over the soft skin of her hand before he let go.

She gazed up at him, those wide brown eyes so damn innocent.

"I don't like it either, but what am I supposed to do? I left him there passed out drunk yesterday, hadn't heard from him all day, and then came home from work to find him here. I've told him it's over, and he just keeps coming back."

"You're doing everything right," Mason assured her. "You'll probably have to cut off all contact. Don't answer the door for him, don't answer his calls. Don't send him any texts. The next step is going to the police though. A restraining order won't keep away someone bound and determined to be here, but it's a start. It'll be official that way."

"The police?" she asked, her eyes widening slightly. "I don't want to get him in some sort of trouble. And it's not like he's done something wrong. I mean nothing illegal anyway."

"Refusing to leave someone alone is stalking them."

"He's not stalking me," she protested.

Mason raised his eyebrows.

"It's not like he's following me around at night, hiding in the shadows or something. He was at my front door!"

"Showing up uninvited again and again is

stalking," he said in a low voice. "Refusing to leave you alone. Not taking no for an answer. Didn't you say you've missed work because of this? He came over and you didn't want to leave?"

"Yeah, but I was afraid to leave him there alone because he was drunk. It's not like he forced me to stay or something."

"Maybe right now he just wants to talk or try to win you back, but what if this escalates? What if he comes over and won't leave? Or if he won't let you leave?"

"Well," she hedged, shifting nervously from foot to foot.

"Is he up there?" Mason asked, nodding his chin toward the stairs.

"He hasn't come down, so I assume so."

"What floor are you on?"

"Third floor. Apartment 307."

"All right. I'll drag him out of the way if I have to. If you don't want to involve the police at this point, we can call a cab or one of his friends to come get him. He'll be pissed as hell if he wakes up feet from your front door. I'm not sure what other options we have. I could have my friends come and take him somewhere."

"Your friends? I don't want to get them in trouble. Besides, it's embarrassing that my ex keeps coming around."

"You have nothing to be embarrassed about. He's the one in the wrong here. Let's go see where he is."

Mason turned and started up the stairs, Taylor following behind. He didn't like that her ex was manipulating her. She was so concerned for his welfare, she didn't want to involve the police.

But hell.

Guys like him just didn't get it.

He reached the landing and crossed to her apartment in a couple long strides. Crouching down by her ex, he frowned. His eyes narrowed at the crushed flowers, but he didn't say anything, just gripped him beneath his arms and dragged him roughly down the hall.

The guy was big—not nearly as muscular as Mason, but he could easily overpower Taylor if he wanted.

Too easily.

Eric continued to lightly snore but didn't stir. Mason unceremoniously dumped him by the top of the stairwell. Crossing back to Taylor's door, he grabbed the empty beer can and flowers.

"Where's the trash?"

"Downstairs."

He nodded and quickly jogged down, flinging the offending items into the trash can. A few moments later and he was back upstairs, walking over to Taylor.

"I can call the police. You can file a report and get this thing rolling tonight."

She shifted nervously. "I'd rather just call someone to get him."

Mason nodded, not happy with her answer. What choice did he have though? If he called them against her wishes, was he any better than this guy? The decision needed to be hers. She needed to feel like she was the one in control around him. "Do you have the number of any of his friends?"

"Yeah. The guy that has my car actually."

Mason pulled out his cell phone and took a picture of Eric lying there by the stairwell.

"Let me see your phone," Mason said.

Taylor looked at him questionably but handed it over.

"What's his friend's name?" After Taylor responded, he sent a text from his own phone. "I just sent him a picture and told him to come get his friend."

Taylor laughed, looking slightly more relaxed. "Won't he wonder who you are?"

Mason shrugged, grabbing her hand. "Don't know, don't care. He can text me back. Let's go inside. His buddy will probably be pissed as hell to have to come get him this late. But if he shows up at your door, I'll be there. We might have a discussion about your car, too."

Taylor nodded, and Mason pulled her close. "I'm glad you texted me earlier."

She slid the key into her lock and pushed open the door. "Well I'm not. I mean I'm glad that you're here, don't get me wrong, but I'd rather not have to deal with any of this at all."

"Understood," Mason said. "I'd rather not have your ex-boyfriend hanging around either."

She crossed the room and turned on a lamp on one of her end tables. Mason's gaze swept the area—the balcony door was locked with a bar down across it. The windows were closed. Good. He turned back and saw that she'd fastened the deadbolt on the front door.

He relaxed slightly, moving further into her apartment.

The space was small but tidy. Small aspects of her personality showed through in the way she'd decorated the space. There were photographs of ocean sunrises on her wall, a basket of seashells on her coffee table. Books were stacked in a neat pile—both fiction and romance, he noted with a grin.

Hell if he wouldn't love to show her a little romance and sweep her off her feet.

Not that now was the appropriate time.

"Did you take those yourself?" he asked, nodding at the mounted photos on the wall.

"I did," she said, her eyes lighting up. "It's a hobby of mine, but I've always loved photography and the ocean."

"They're amazing," he said, walking closer to get a better look. "You must've been up really early to take these. I've seen plenty of sunrises in my days in the Navy—not usually by choice."

She laughed, the melodious sound sending electricity coursing through him. "Yep. I try to avoid getting up that early normally. I can't resist a good sunrise though."

"Duly noted," he said, a smile tugging at the corner of his mouth.

Wouldn't he love to enjoy a sunrise with her. Preferably after getting to know her all night.

Taylor dropped her purse onto an armchair and crossed over to stand at his side. She yawned, blushing again as he chuckled.

"It's late," he said, briefly letting his fingers trail down her bare arm. "I'm sure you're exhausted. Just grab me a blanket or something, and I'll crash on the sofa."

"Are you sure?" she asked. "I mean, I could stay out here and let you have the bed. You're a lot taller than me."

"Sweetheart, I'm a Navy SEAL. I've slept in tents

pitched in the desert," he said with a grin. "The hard floor of a C-17 cargo plane on a nonstop flight across the Atlantic. Believe me when I say your sofa is a luxury compared to any of that. And hell, your company is infinitely better than that of my buddies. You're much better looking than them, too."

She blushed furiously, and he smiled.

"I'm not trying to make you uncomfortable. This wasn't exactly a planned date or something. You relax, do whatever you need to do, and I'll be out here. Tomorrow I'll go home and change and then we'll go out on a proper date. I'll come pick you up and everything."

"If you're sure," she hedged.

"About the date?"

"About sleeping out here."

Mason's phone buzzed with an incoming text, and he pulled it from his pocket.

Who the fuck is this?

Mason frowned and thumbed a response.

A friend of Taylor's. Tell her ex not to come around here anymore.

"What's wrong?" Taylor asked, noticing the expression on his face.

"It's that guy Jake. He wondered who was texting him—no surprise. I didn't say anything earlier, just told him to get his friend."

"Is Eric still out there?" Taylor asked, moving toward her front door.

"I'll check," Mason said, holding his hand up to stop her. She froze in place, and something in his chest warmed as he crossed the room. She trusted him. Listened to him. He was used to being in control, and she had enough faith in him to let him be.

He knew she was independent in many ways, living alone, keeping a waitressing job that gave her time for pursuing her hobbies. But the fact that she'd let him into her space and let him take control of the situation spoke volumes.

He loved to be in command—both in and out of the bedroom. The fact that she was willing to let him be so far spoke well for their future.

And hell, what was he doing thinking about their future?

He still hadn't even taken her out yet. Kissed her goodnight.

Somehow he knew he'd do whatever it took to keep her happy and safe though.

Mason peered through the peephole, his hand on the doorknob. "Nope, he's already gone. Either he left himself or his friend came."

"Probably Jake already came. He lives close by."

"Damn. I would've liked a word with him, too."

"Another time," she said. "Maybe tomorrow we can get my car back. I mean, if you don't mind coming with me. I'm tired of calling and asking about it. Eric's friend just keeps giving me the runaround."

"Absolutely," he assured her. "Are they open on Sundays?"

Her face fell. "Actually, I don't think so."

"No problem. I'll go with you to get it—first thing Monday morning if we have to. We'll handle it."

She nodded, looking nervous, then gathered a blanket and pillow and placed them on the sofa. "Are you sure you don't mind staying over? I mean, Eric's already gone, so there's no need…."

"There's no where else I'd rather be," he assured

her. "I want to make sure you're safe."

His eyes heated for a moment as he walked over to stand by her side. This wasn't exactly how he'd imagined his first night with her would go, but he liked knowing where she was. Safe. Home. With him.

Maybe he wouldn't be taking her to bed just yet, but crashing outside her bedroom door was a hell of a lot better than pitching a tent with his buddies.

He wrapped his arms around her, pulling her in for a hug. Inhaling her sunshiny scent. She relaxed against him, sighing in contentment. "Sweet dreams, Taylor," he said, brushing his lips over her hair. "You don't have to worry about anything when I'm here."

Chapter 8

The sound of pounding on her front door jolted Taylor out of a deep slumber. In a flash, she was sitting up in bed, her heart racing. A cold sweat broke out over her skin, and her eyes landed on the clock on her nightstand.

3:08 a.m.

Rubbing sleep from her eyes, she stood, forgetting for a moment that she had on only her skimpy camisole and shorts. She hurried to her bedroom door, nearly tripping over her own two feet as she remembered Mason was out there sleeping on her sofa.

Mason, who had the body of a Greek God. Who probably rolled out of bed looking perfect.

She felt like a rumpled mess, but the pounding on her front door continued.

Mason flicked on a light, meeting her gaze, and then he was crossing her living room. Taking a quick glance out through her peephole before cracking the door.

"Don't come here again," he said in cool voice.

"Who the fuck are you?" Eric's voice came from the other side of the door. He said something else, slurring his words, and Taylor realized he was still drunk.

"None of your damn business. If I see you around here again, the police will be the least of your concerns."

"Let me inside. Where's Taylor?"

"Eric!" another male voice shouted from outside. "What the hell are you doing here? Give me my damn keys!"

Taylor heard a scuffle, and then Mason stepped further into the doorway, bodily blocking her view. She hurried over to the door, hesitating.

If she went out there, it would only make things worse. Eric would see her and lose his mind.

As it were, Mason clearly didn't want her outside. His large body was blocking her way.

"Are you the guy who has Taylor's car?" Mason asked, irritated. "We'll be picking it up tomorrow."

Jake's voice carried into her apartment through open door.

"Sorry man," Jake said smugly. "It's not ready. And we're not even open on Sundays."

"How the hell can it not be ready? You've had it for over a week. After what you charged Taylor for a tow last month, I assume the repairs are free of charge."

"We just need to order a part."

"Order it," Mason demanded. "I'll expect an update on Monday morning as to when we can pick it up."

"Who is that guy?" Eric slurred.

"Nobody. Let's go," Jake said. "I've got enough problems without chasing you over here twice in one goddamn night."

"Monday," Mason repeated, closing the door before either of them could respond.

Taylor let out a breath she hadn't even realized she was holding. She stepped back, watching as Mason turned the deadbolt. For someone that had been sound asleep like her, he sure the heck looked wide-eyed and alert. The fact that he was fully dressed while she had on her sleep shorts and camisole might have had something to do with it.

He turned to face her, his eyes heating as he glanced down at her lavender pajamas.

Although she was fully covered, she suddenly felt naked under his observant gaze. She felt feminine and small next to him. Fragile. He was all muscle, brawn, and bravado, and she couldn't even get her ex-boyfriend to leave her alone.

"Are you okay?" he asked, his blue eyes locking with hers.

"Fine."

"You're shaking," he said softly, taking a step closer.

Heat licked through her as her gaze slid over his broad shoulders, trailing down his muscled chest. She could only imagine the washboard abs beneath his tee shirt, but oh, wouldn't that be a sight to see.

"I just—it caught me off guard. What if you hadn't been here? He was pounding on my door, demanding to come inside…."

Much to her utter embarrassment, tears sprang to

her eyes.

"Taylor, sweetheart," he said, stepping closer and gathering her to him. She let out a muffled sob and collapsed into his embrace, the weight of his muscular arms wrapping around her.

He was solid and safe. Warm.

It felt as if nothing bad could ever happen to her when Mason was here.

The heat of his hands seared into the bare flesh of her back, his rough fingertips dragging over her skin where the skimpy straps of her camisole lay.

She was next-to-naked, vulnerable, and had never felt so safe.

He pulled her even closer, and she inhaled his scent of soap and spice. He was pure male—so masculine it almost hurt. The opposite of her in every way.

And he'd rushed over tonight for her.

But wasn't that exactly the problem? Mason couldn't always be here. They weren't even together for goodness sakes. He'd come for her tonight, yes, but wouldn't always be around. Fresh tears spilled down her cheeks, and then suddenly Mason was lifting her into his arms. Carrying her into her bedroom.

He cradled her close, like she was something fragile to be taken care of and cherished.

"Shh, sweetheart. You're safe. I'm right here."

He padded across her room in the darkness, only the glow from her clock on the nightstand and light from the living room showing him the way.

It felt intimate to have him hold her this way.

To have Mason here in her bedroom.

His strength and warmth surrounded her, and she

inhaled his scent. He lay her down on the bed, and she refused to let go, pulling him right down beside her, enjoying the feeling of his body beside hers. She continued to cry quietly into his chest as he held her, his muscular arms tightening, and finally her tears began to slow.

"Shh," he said again, his hand stroking over her hair.

She hugged him even tighter. "Stay with me," she whispered.

"I'm right here," he assured her. "I'll hold you all night."

***

Taylor mumbled as she began to wake, her body wrapped around something warm and solid. She nestled closer, hovering at that delicious moment between sleep and wakefulness, her entire body relaxed.

She felt safe in her little cocoon, content.

She wanted to hold onto this feeling of lightness. Of slumber. Of being safe and warm where nothing bad could ever happen to her.

She shifted slightly as her sex throbbed, and with a gasp, she realized her leg was over Mason's muscular thigh, her arms wrapped around him, her head on his chest. He was just beginning to stir himself, still wearing his tee shirt and shorts from the night before, but there was no mistaking the bulge in his shorts.

Inches away from her leg.

She moved again, her silken legs skimming over his muscular ones. The springy hair on his legs tickled her skin, and there was something erotic about awaking this way, her body against his, their legs intertwined. Mason's arms still wrapped around her.

He'd held her as she fell asleep last night, but somehow she'd nestled even closer to him throughout the night.

Curled her entire body around his so that she was clinging to him.

His arms shifted as he began to wake up, his fingers lazily trailing over her bare skin.

The drag of his hands over her silken camisole and skin felt good.

Too good.

For a man she still hadn't even been out on a date with, he was holding her in his arms like they were meant to be together.

"Hell, this feels good," he mumbled. "I like waking up with you in my arms."

"Me too," she said, flushing.

She could hear his heartbeat thumping beneath his chest, the soft cotton of his tee shirt pressed against her cheek. Mason's hands continued moving, caressing her gently. Her camisole rode up slightly, and then his hands were on her bare skin, his thumb just edging beneath the bottom of her top.

A fresh wave of heat rushed though her at his touch. Her heart thumped in her chest as she imagined him pulling her on top of him, thrusting inside her, their bodies naked and intertwined.

Neither of them said anything for a beat, and then she finally lifted herself up to meet his gaze. His eyes dropped to her cleavage, perfectly on display for him in her delicate camisole. "You're beautiful," he said in a low voice. "Gorgeous."

Her sharp intake of breath was her only response,

and then Mason was slowly lifting her up until she was straddling him. His erection nudged against her swollen sex, her legs spread over his hips. Even though she was atop him she felt frozen in place. Unable to move away from the feeling of his thick length running along her core.

He captured the back of her neck with one large hand, and then he was guiding her toward him for a kiss.

Despite the fact that he was stretched out on her bed and she was literally sitting on top of him, Mason remained in complete and utter control.

Commanding the situation even with her above him.

Her heart fluttered as he moved closer, and then at last her lips met his.

His kiss was soft and gentle, but one of his hands moved back to her hip, gripping her in place. Holding her exactly where she wanted to be.

Even through his shorts, she could feel him. Was intimately aware of how big he was. Arousal dampened her folds, and she blushed, realizing how wet she'd become. Her chest heaved as he kissed her again, deeper, and she bucked lightly against him.

Taking her lead, he nudged his cock against her as she gasped.

Trembling, she sat up, slowly lifting her camisole up and over her head. Baring herself to him.

"Taylor, what are you doing?" he asked, his voice gravel.

"Throwing caution to the wind."

His hands rose to her breasts, kneading and caressing. His thumbs skated across her nipples, causing her to whimper in pleasure. And then he was pushing himself up. Sucking one of her nipples into his mouth. She gasped as pure pleasure shot straight through her. His tongue flickered over her nipple, hot, wet, and perfect as he teased and tormented her.

Pleasure shot straight to her clit, and she arched her back, thrusting her breasts even closer to him.

Feeling like she might spontaneously combust right there and then.

Mason laved his tongue over her, kissing his way around her areola.

And then before she even knew what was happening, he was rolling them both over. Hovering above her.

Muscular arms came down on either side of her head, effectively caging her on. He nudged apart her thighs with one knee and ducked lower.

His teeth grazed the delicate skin of her neck as he moved back down her body, one large hand palming her breast. He groaned in appreciation, and then his mouth shortly followed. He licked her nipple, watching it pebble further beneath his touch, before sucking it back into his mouth. Lightly biting down on her taut bud.

"Mason!" she cried out.

He blew on her gently, soothing the sting, before giving her other breast equal treatment.

Taylor whimpered and moaned beneath him, completely lost to his touch. Completely lost in him.

His hands moved reverently over her, caressing her skin with gentle touches. Hot lips followed in their path, setting her ablaze. Making her entire body light up with warmth.

One large hand cupped her sex, his finger deftly sliding along her slit through the silken material of her pajama shorts.

"Hell you're wet, sweetheart," he said appreciatively. "I can feel you even through these sexy little shorts you have on."

His thick finger trailed over her again, and then he was rubbing her clit through the silken material. Causing her to cry out in pleasure.

His mouth returned to one breast, sucking it into his mouth, and his thick fingers slid under her shorts, parting her silken folds. She was dripping in arousal, her sex swollen with need. Mason wasted no time as she moaned, just slid his fingers up through her folds and expertly circled her clit with one fingertip.

She whimpered beneath him, the touch too soft to do anything but tease her.

To make her want to beg and plead with him for more.

His finger circled faster as he applied more pressure, and then she was arching against him, her cries louder. His tongue flickered mercilessly against her nipple, his hand moving faster and faster over her clit.

Shockwaves of pleasure began to spark within her. Pinpoints of light in an otherwise dark abyss. Every aspect of her existence hinged on his touch. There was nothing else—no one else. Her whole world was Mason.

He lightly bit down on her nipple, rubbing her clit faster, and she screamed, finally falling over the edge of the precipice she'd been balancing on.

Explosions of pure pleasure clouded her vision, and as he expertly continued his ministrations, her orgasm went on and on.

Mason eased her back down from her release,

softly rubbing her sex with his hand.

Finally, as she lay panting and sated, he withdrew his hand from her arousal-dampened folds. Bringing his fingers to his mouth, glistening with her juices, he tasted her.

Taylor watched in awe as he grinned, looking like the cat that had just caught the canary.

"You taste so damn good, Taylor. Next time I want you to come on my tongue. I can't wait to have my mouth all over you."

He stood up from her bed, adjusting himself in his shorts.

She sat up, pulling the covers up to cover her breasts. "But you—you're…." She trailed off. Didn't he want her to reciprocate? Or for them to have sex? He'd given her the most amazing orgasm of her entire life and now was standing up in her bedroom like it was just the start of another day.

"Another time, sweetheart. This was just about you. For you."

"Mason—oh my God," she said, closing her eyes.

He chuckled and ducked down for a kiss. "I liked having you come apart in my arms," he said huskily. The back of his fingers brushed over her flushed cheek. She opened her eyes and gazed up into his bright blue ones.

"You don't know how many times I've imagined that in my mind."

"You've…thought about us?" Heat bloomed within her chest. Goodness knew she'd thought about Mason enough. But just because he'd asked her out didn't necessarily mean she was always on his mind.

Hearing the words straight from his mouth though—she beamed up at him.

"Hell yes, sweetheart. Many times. And when I woke up hard as a rock with you wrapped around me this morning, I couldn't imagine anything better. I know you wanted to take things slowly with me, but this morning was pretty damn perfect."

"God, last night," she said with a groan, briefly covering her eyes with one hand. She dropped it back down to the sheets as she looked at Mason. "I can't believe Eric came back here. Again. I mean, if you weren't here, he probably would've just kept pounding on my door."

Mason nodded, his face grim. "You're going to have to call the police, Taylor. Start documenting every time he shows up."

"Yeah. You're right. It's starting to get out of hand."

He scrubbed a hand across his jaw. "I know you're still without a car. Want to get ready and I'll take you to the police station?"

"I'll call and file a report later this morning. I think they can send an officer to me."

"I meant what I said about getting your car back tomorrow."

"I know, I just don't think it'll be ready."

Mason ducked down and grabbed her silky camisole from the floor, handing it to her. "Then I'll be giving him a call every day for an update."

Taylor clutched her camisole in one hand, nervously looking up at Mason. He'd seen her breasts already, touched her intimately.

Tasted her, she thought with a blush.

Why did dressing in front of him embarrass her?

"Here," he said, holding his hand out to her. She took his hand and rose from the bed as Mason ducked down and kissed her, his free hand lightly running over the side of one breast. "You look sexy as hell topless, but I want you to feel comfortable."

She let him help her slide the camisole back on, the bulge in his pants as prominent as ever. "I'm going to need a very cold shower when I get home."

"Mason," she protested, reaching out for him.

"Another time. This was about you, remember?"

She nodded, looking at him in confusion. Maybe he didn't want her to touch him? Clearly he was aroused. A mixture of thoughts warred within her.

"I'll come back and pick you up in a few hours for our date. Sound okay?" he asked.

"Oh, uh, sure," she said.

"If Eric or his buddy come back here before then, call 911. Then call me. I'll come over immediately. But make sure you file that police report this morning."

"Okay I will."

"I don't like leaving you here alone," Mason said. "Not without a way to leave."

"This has been going on for several weeks," she said with a shrug. "I don't like it either, but hopefully getting the police involved will be enough to keep them from coming back."

"I can bring you to my place if you'd feel more comfortable."

"Mason," she said with a sigh. "I can't hide from my ex. I need to live my own life. And even though it's annoying and creepy that he keeps coming over, he hasn't threatened me or hurt me. I'll be fine."

He nodded, his mouth in a grim line. "All right. I'll be back in a few hours, okay?"

"Okay."

He leaned down and brushed his lips across her forehead then turned to go. She stood there for a moment, flustered, and then followed him into her living room.

"Lock the door behind me," he said as he turned the deadbolt.

"I always do," she assured him.

He turned in the doorway, his large body shielding her from the hallway outside. "No need to let the neighbors see you in that," he said, his eyes heating.

Her nipples pebbled beneath his gaze, and the corner of his mouth tugged up in a smile. "See you soon, sweetheart."

"See you soon," she said, closing the door behind him.

Heat bloomed over her skin as memories of their morning flashed through her mind. Mason was sexy as sin, and she'd just let him pleasure her in her bed. She had no idea what he had planned for their afternoon together, but not even a minute had gone by since he'd left, and she already missed him.

Chapter 9

Mason drummed his fingers on the steering wheel an hour later as he drove down the highway, headed to meet Hunter at Little Creek for a game of one-on-one.

He flashed his military ID at the gate, nodding at the guards. A few minutes later he was pulling into an empty parking space and climbing out of his SUV. He grabbed his basketball, water canteen, and a spare towel from the trunk, slamming it shut, and walked back toward the edge of base where the guys liked to play ball.

Hell.

His mind had been going a million miles a minute since he woke up this morning. Since he'd hurried over to Taylor's last night. He hadn't liked leaving her alone earlier, but what was he supposed to do?

He'd spent the night. Kissed her. Pleasured her.

Admired her gorgeous breasts and felt the heat of

her against his cock as she'd straddled him.

Then he'd jumped up out of bed before he took things too far. Before he'd tugged down those satiny shorts, the delicate fabric the only thing separating her from him. Before he'd freed his aching erection and claimed her right then and there.

Mason wanted them to go out on a proper first date, without the distraction of her ex or his friends or anyone else around.

He wanted to show her that she was important to him. That he wasn't just looking for a quick lay.

The image of her sitting astride him, lifting that skimpy little camisole over her head would be forever emblazoned in his memory though. She had perfect, full breasts with rosy, round nipples. He'd been shocked by her boldness—Taylor was always blushing and quiet around him.

Looking away if his gaze was too intense.

The fact that she'd been comfortable enough to partially strip in front of him spoke volumes. She'd looked almost hurt when he hadn't wanted her to reciprocate, but hell. He wanted to take her out. Take his time getting to know her better, hearing her laugh and watching the rosiness spread over her cheeks.

And then spend an entire night exploring her body.

Kissing her and pleasuring her before finally working up to claiming her as his.

It had taken everything in him not to free his aching cock from his shorts earlier. Not to lift her up and then pull her back down on top of him, allowing him to sink straight into heaven.

"No one else could make it?" Hunter asked, cocking his brow as Mason sauntered over to the court.

Mason dropped his towel and water to the ground. "Negative. Guess those guys were out late and had better things to do this morning."

Hunter smirked. "No surprise—they're all single. Except for Colton, but I'm sure Camila is keeping him occupied. Which begs the question of what you're doing up so bright and early on a Sunday morning. Shouldn't you have taken a pretty lady home last night as well?"

"I was with Taylor," Mason said, cutting right to the chase.

Hunter raised his eyebrows. "With her as in you spent the night? Then what the hell are you doing here?"

Mason chuckled. "Shouldn't I ask the same of you? Last I checked you had a woman yourself keeping your bed warm."

"Yep. But Emma's getting ready for some reading at a bookstore in Williamsburg this morning."

"On a Sunday?"

Hunter shrugged. "I guess its popular with the academic crowd over there."

Mason nodded. There were several colleges local to the Virginia Beach area, and Williamsburg was only an hour away. Emma had started guest lecturing at The College of William and Mary after moving from London to Virginia Beach.

"I offered to come, but I think she prefers if I don't," Hunter added with a chuckle. "It's some archeologist reading about his latest archeological dig. Much more Emma's cup of tea—pun intended. She knows I don't particularly enjoy sitting through those things."

Mason snorted. "Cup of tea? Hell man, you're starting to sound like her. What's next? Sharing make-up tips?"

"I'll let her know you're interested," Hunter ribbed him.

"Is she going on any more digs soon?"

"Not if I have anything to say about it," Hunter grumbled. He'd met Emma in London after she'd gotten back from a trip to the Middle East. She'd accidentally stumbled on some information a terrorist cell was after, and they'd chased her from London all the way to the States to obtain the documents.

"I hear you, man." Mason grabbed the basketball and began dribbling, moving around on the court. "Wait until Emma hears that you think her lectures are boring," he added with a chuckle. "I can't see that going over well."

"She doesn't have to wait to hear it—she already knows it. Luckily we're compatible in other areas."

Mason snorted, jumping and shooting the ball through the air. The chemistry between Hunter and Emma had always been red hot, and he had no doubt they set things afire between the sheets.

Hell.

If his morning with Taylor was any indication, their bedroom would combust when they finally made love for the first time.

The basketball he'd shot sailed through the net with a swoosh, and Mason grinned.

"So what was the deal with Taylor?" Hunter asked. "You up and ran out on her this morning?"

Something in Mason's chest tightened. He had sort of done that, hadn't he? But he was seeing her later on. And he'd rushed out the door to keep things from going too far. To keep her from regretting anything.

When he had her for the first time, he wanted her to be one hundred percent sure. Not because she'd woken up wrapped around his body after he'd rushed over in the middle of the night.

It's not like he'd taken what he wanted and left.

He'd given her some space. Kept their plans for their date later on.

"I went over there because her ex showed up again last night," Mason said. "Taylor got home from work, and he was passed out at her door."

"Hell," Hunter muttered. "The guy can't take no for an answer, huh?"

"Negative. I had to drag his sorry ass out of there just so she could get in her apartment. I crashed on the couch in case he came back, and sure enough, he was pounding on her door in the middle of the night. Thank God I was there, because she probably would've felt guilty and let him in."

"I'm surprised the neighbors didn't call the cops."

Mason shrugged, rebounding Hunter's shot.

They'd abandoned their one-on-one game just for shooting the breeze. He dribbled the ball, frowning. "I told Taylor to go to the police last night. She didn't want to but said she would this morning. I think her ex showing up in the middle of the night spooked her. Hopefully it was what she needed to make the call."

Hunter nodded, glancing over at Mason. "She's not the first woman to be stalked by an ex. She needs to stop this before it escalates. Showing up again and again is bad enough."

"Exactly my concern," Mason agreed. "Remember when Taylor was late to work Friday night? It's because her ex was over there then, too. He showed up drunk, and she let him in."

"Sounds like he's taking advantage of the situation."

"You know it, I know it, her neighbors probably all know it. The problem is, until Taylor sees it that way, she's going to keep feeling sorry for him and letting him into her apartment. I'm hoping last night convinced her otherwise, but hell. If I hadn't been there crashing on her sofa, I have a feeling she would've just let him in again. And one of these days he's going to want more than just coming into her apartment."

"So you spent the night at a woman's place but didn't sleep with her?" Hunter asked with a smirk. "Doesn't sound like you, Riptide," he said, calling him by his nickname.

"Not in the manner you're thinking, asshole. Get your mind out of the gutter."

"So you were in her bed," Hunter said with a chuckle.

Mason threw the basketball him, and Hunter easily palmed it in one large hand, shooting it at the net. "You've got a one-track mind," Mason muttered.

"Emma doesn't have a problem with it," Hunter said with a grin. "She rather enjoys all the attention."

"Hell, you guys started off with a bang. Taylor and I have been dancing around each other forever. If I had it my way, we would've gone out months ago."

"She was dating that asshole," Hunter said.

"Yep. But they broke up a month ago. And we're finally going out this afternoon."

"How sweet," Hunter quipped. "A little afternoon delight?"

Mason flipped him off before taking a jump shot, the ball neatly gliding into the net. Hell. Hadn't he just been here with his buddies the other night for a game before a round of beers? It was amazing how quickly things had changed in a matter of days.

They played for another hour, Hunter besting Mason in a game of one-on-one.

"All right, I'll catch you later," Mason finally said, grabbing the ball as it rolled back toward him. "I need to shower and change before I head back to Taylor's place to pick her up."

"Enjoy your date, lover boy."

"I plan to," Mason said with a smirk. "But don't worry, I'll spare you all the details."

***

Taylor opened the door an hour later, her entire face lighting up as Mason grinned at her. She had on a sundress and strappy little sandals and clutched a lightweight sweater in one hand.

"Is this okay?" she asked nervously. "You said dress for the outdoors, but I wasn't sure if I needed to be more casual."

"It's perfect," Mason said appreciatively. "You look gorgeous."

And she did. The floral sundress was pretty and feminine, and the fabric in the front criss-crossed over her chest. It wasn't mean to be revealing, but the overall look was sexy as hell. It was like her breasts had been wrapped up in a pretty little package just for him to admire.

The dress was slightly loose, falling to mid-thigh, and Mason felt his groin tighten as Taylor turned to grab her purse.

The delicate fabric dancing over her silky thighs was going to be the death of him.

He'd felt all her soft skin this morning. Parted her legs and touched her silken folds. He'd thought of nothing else but running his hands all over her beautiful body ever since.

Touching her. Teasing her. Watching her reactions as he explored all of her gorgeous curves.

And now to have her wearing a sexy little dress that teased and tempted him?

It was going to be a long afternoon.

She pulled the door shut and locked it, soft curls bouncing around her face. She must've done something to her hair because usually it was long and straight. Normally he didn't care much about hair or make-up, thinking it made a woman look overly done, like she was trying too hard.

But on Taylor?

She looked even softer and more feminine.

Not to mention sexy as sin.

"I thought we'd have a picnic down on the quiet end of the beach," he said as they walked down her stairwell. "Sound okay?"

"That sounds perfect."

"I already packed a picnic blanket and food. I like the idea of us having an afternoon alone together, but the next time we have a bonfire on the beach with my friends, I want to bring you, too."

"You guys have bonfires?"

He nodded, unlocking the door to his SUV. His hands wrapped around her slender waist as he helped her climb in, and he resisted the urge to groan. She smelled amazing—her usual combination of sunshine and coconut, plus an underlying floral scent. Was it a new perfume or something?

His cock hardened as he imagined stripping her down, discovering the source of that intoxicating aroma. Hell if he couldn't spend hours exploring her body.

He helped her fasten the seatbelt, his large hand briefly resting on her bare thigh. Her skin was so soft and smooth compared to his, he resisted the urge to run his hand up and down it.

"The other SEAL team on base gets together a lot, and we started joining them sometimes. I'd love to bring you along and introduce you to the others. You've met the guys on my team, but the Alpha SEAL team is all married or attached. You'd like the other women."

She nodded, looking slightly nervous.

"Hell, sweetheart, there's nothing to worry about. They'll all love you. And today it's just you and me."

His thumb lightly grazed over the skin of her thigh, and he watched in fascination as heat bloomed over her skin. Unable to resist, he ducked down, kissing her softly. She tasted of strawberries and something else sweet. He wanted to deepen the kiss and pull her close, but here in the parking lot wasn't exactly the best place.

Besides, she was already buckled in.

A slight breeze blew in from the ocean as he reluctantly stood back up, and he grinned, inhaling the salty sea air. "This is the perfect time of year to enjoy the beach—not too hot and humid but still warm enough to relax and stretch out on the sand."

"Exactly. I'm down there nearly every day. That's partly why I love working at Anchors."

"I thought it was because you get to see me," he said with a wink.

She flushed again, and the corner of his lip quirked up in a smile. "Go on, sweetheart. You know I love teasing you."

"I just meant I like having my days free."

"I totally understand. I could never have a desk job for that very reason. We're out training and drilling in all weather, but days like today make it all worth it."

He closed her door and walked around the front of the SUV, climbing into the driver's seat. There was something that felt right about having Taylor sitting in the passenger seat. That flirty little dress grazed her thighs, her chest rose and fell slightly, the tendrils of her hair curling around her breasts, framing them perfectly. He wanted nothing more than to reach over and pick up one strand, running it between his fingers.

To kiss the side of her neck, inhaling her sweetness, and work his way down.

"I'm going to take you to the beach one morning and watch the sun rise," he said, his voice gruff. "Preferably after I've held you in my arms all night."

She flushed again, and male pride surged through him. He loved the effect that he had on her. Couldn't wait to fully have her. He'd been with plenty of women over the years, but a lot of those one-night-stands and short-term relationships were too easy. Too casual.

Maybe they provided some immediate, instant satisfaction, but having Taylor would be different.

She didn't seem like the type of woman who slept around.

Hell. Hadn't she said she'd dated that last jackass for several years?

He couldn't wait to claim her fully. Completely. To lay her down in his bed, part her creamy thighs, and thrust into her, driving so deep he wouldn't know where he stopped and she began.

Hearing her cries of pleasure this morning had made him feel ten feet tall. Had made him want to claim her again and again. To have her come on his cock, his tongue—he couldn't imagine anything better.

Couldn't wait to have all of her.

"I'd like that," she said shyly.

"Like to watch the sunrise with me? Or like for me to hold you all night?"

"Yes. Both," she quickly amended, and Mason chuckled.

"You don't need to be nervous around me," he said quietly.

"I know—I just feel flustered. You say exactly what you're thinking, and I just don't know what to do with that."

"I'll always be honest with you," Mason said.

"I appreciate it. It's just different than what I'm used to."

"It sounds like your ex didn't treat you right," Mason said with a grumble. "Which reminds me. Did you call the police earlier?"

"Yeah, I did," she said, nodding. "An officer came and took a report. A neighbor of mine happened to be coming home right then, and she said she's seen Eric hanging around here when I'm not home. I guess he was coming more than I realized—I'm stuck at home more now without a car."

Mason clenched his jaw, nodding as he started the engine. "We'll remedy that this week, sweetheart. And I'll get you the numbers for the rest of the guys on my team. The other team, too. I want to make sure you can reach them in case of an emergency."

Taylor bit her lip, looking frustrated.

"How about we forget about him for a while and just enjoy us," Mason said, reaching over and taking her much smaller hand in his. Her hand was so delicate and smooth. He lazily traced circles over the back of it was his thumb, his other hand firmly on the steering wheel.

"Now that I can get on board with," she said with a relieved sigh. "I'm tired of letting him dictate my life."

Mason pulled onto the road, heading away from the busy tourist stretch of the beach.

They passed another beach community, but before long they were in a more secluded area. Mason pulled his SUV to a stop, cutting the engine. The small sandy parking area off the road wasn't a real parking lot, but the locals came here a lot to enjoy the private section of the beach.

There were no other cars around today, and Mason loved that he and Taylor would be alone. "I packed a ton of things for lunch since I didn't know what you liked," he said.

"I'm not picky," she assured him as she shifted to unfasten her seatbelt. Mason's groin tightened as her dress slid slightly higher up her bare thighs.

Hell.

Every little thing she did he found sexy.

The way her curls fell down over her shoulders. The way she moved. The way her chocolate brown eyes widened as she looked at him.

She flushed slightly as she caught him watching her.

"You look beautiful," he said. Not wanted to make her uncomfortable, he held her gaze for a moment and climbed out and rounded the SUV, opening her door. He took her hand and helped her step out, letting his hand linger on her waist as he moved to assist her.

He towered above her, loving the way her small body fit against his. He brushed some of her hair back from her face as the ocean breeze blew. "I like your hair like this," he said, capturing one curl between his finger and thumb. "You always wear it straight, but this looks incredible."

"I'll probably have to pull it back since we're at the beach. It'll be blowing in my face all afternoon."

"Damn. I should've told you ahead of time where we're going."

"It's fine," she assured him. "And I love the ocean."

"Duly noted," he said with a grin, moving toward the trunk of his SUV. He opened the back hatch and grabbed his backpack laden with food and drinks and a soft blanket that he'd stashed beside it. "I don't have an actual picnic basket. This'll work though," he said, turning back toward her as he swung the backpack onto his back.

Taylor had already pulled a hair tie out of her bag and was pulling her hair back into some type of twist. Her slender neck was elongated, and he saw she had on some dangly earrings he hadn't even noticed earlier.

The glint of silver caught in the sunlight. A few

stray pieces of her hair fell loose, but it gave her a softer appearance.

Hell, he wanted to tug her hair back down and run his fingers through it, kissing her senseless here in the parking area. Back her against his SUV and feel her curves against him.

That would have to wait though.

He brought her out here to enjoy lunch and an afternoon down at the ocean, not to make out with her on the side of the road.

"Let's go," he said, tucking the blanket under one arm so he could take her hand with the other.

"Can I carry something?" she asked, looking over at him.

"Not a chance."

She laughed, the light, musical sound filling his chest with warmth. "You do know I usually carry my own things to the beach," she said, sounding amused. "Beach chairs, towels, coolers—you name it. Not to mention lugging my photography equipment around when I'm wanting to capture some decent photographs."

"I know, and I also know you don't need to when I'm here."

"But that's silly," she protested.

"Hell, sweetheart, it's nothing. I plan to do plenty for you when we're together. If you're dating me, there's a lot you won't need to worry about."

"So now we're dating," she teased, glancing up at him. "I thought this was just our first date?"

He pulled her hand to his mouth and brushed his lips across the back of it, loving the way that she shivered at his touch. "The first of many. How about over there?" he asked, nodding his head toward a flat stretch of beach twenty feet away. "It looks like a good spot and far enough back from the tide that our blanket won't get wet."

"It looks perfect," she said.

Mason spread the blanket down on the sand and watched as Taylor elegantly fold her legs beneath her and sat down. Her dress hugged her breasts even more in that position, and he resisted the urge to groan.

He set his backpack down on one corner of the blanket to help weight it down, sinking to the ground beside her.

"All right—I've got sandwiches, fruit, cheese, crackers, water, pretzels."

"Wow, you must be hungry," she said.

"I worked up an appetite this morning," he quipped. "Actually, I really did. I played basketball with Hunter on base after I left your place."

She opened a bottle of water and took a long sip, setting it beside her on the blanket. "Basketball, huh? You're a busy guy."

"Hell, I could've stayed with you all morning, but I wanted to give you some space."

"Yeah, uh, this morning—wow."

Mason chuckled, loving the hint of rosiness that spread across her cheeks. Hell, he'd thought of little else since then. Driving away from her apartment, he'd imagined all the ways he could pleasure her. All the nights and mornings they'd spend making love.

Although he hadn't exactly planned on spending the night at her place, he hoped for a hell of a lot more of that in their future.

"I could go for some fruit and a sandwich," Taylor said, changing the subject.

"Sure thing. I confess that I made none of this," he said with a grin as he started pulling plastic containers from his backpack.

"You didn't make it and then package it like they do at the grocery store? Seriously, Mason, this is perfect. I mean, why do you think I work at Anchors? I love being by the water. And I think its sweet that you packed a picnic for this.

Mason chuckled. "Sweet, huh? Do me a favor and don't tell the rest of my SEAL team."

Taylor smiled at him, the ocean breeze rustling the loose tendrils of her hair. "Don't worry, your secret's safe with me."

"Next time I'll bring a bottle of wine. I wish I thought of it earlier—I kind of just grabbed what I could at the grocery store."

"But you're a beer drinker," she said, taking a bite of her sandwich.

He chuckled. "That I am. I'd probably bring a couple of beers for myself. But, when I bring you to that bonfire I was telling you about, there's always several coolers full of drinks. Most of the guys are beer drinkers, as you know. But the women are more into wine."

"It looks like a storm in the distance," Taylor said, squinting at the horizon.

Mason gazed out at the dark clouds over the ocean. They were several miles away and would probably blow right up the coast. "I think it'll stay offshore. It was supposed to be great weather on the beach today. There are plenty of times there are storms at sea that never come onto the land."

"Have you been caught in any?"

Mason nodded, taking a bite of his own sandwich.

"Hell, we train in them sometimes. Mother Nature doesn't care when we get called up, so we have to be prepared for all kinds of scenarios."

"I guess you can't really talk about the work you do—the missions you go on and stuff."

"That's a negative, sweetheart. And it's not because I'm ever trying to keep something from you. The missions themselves require operational security—we can't risk having word get out as to where we're deploying to, what we're doing, when we'll be back. And even when we return, no one else is privy to the details."

"I understand," she said softly.

"What's wrong?" he asked. "You look a little sad."

She shrugged. "I'll just worry about you when you're gone. I mean—I know we're not exactly dating or something. This is just one date," she hurriedly rambled on.

Mason's chest tightened. She looked so flustered at the moment, but damn. To have someone worry about him back at home when he went out on an op?

It hadn't exactly been something he'd wanted until right at this moment.

And now?

He couldn't imagine leaving without rushing right back to her side when he returned.

Chapter 10

"This isn't just one date, sweetheart. It's our first date."

Taylor smiled, sneaking a glance back over at Mason. "I didn't mean to make the conversation so serious," she said, watching Mason squint in the sunlight as he looked out at the storms in the distance. "We're supposed to be just relaxing and enjoying a picnic lunch."

Mason met her gaze, and she briefly took in his form stretched out on the blanket. Broad shoulders, bulging biceps. A tee shirt that stretched across his impressive chest. His long legs were stretched out in front of him, as muscular and tan as the rest of him. The tiny golden hairs on his arms and legs stood out in the sunlight.

He looked masculine and virile. A bundle of energy captured in a brief moment of respite.

What did he see in a woman like her?

Her life was…boring compared to his. She went to the same place every day—same customers, same food, same old Anchors. She came down to the beach every morning. Loved photographing the ocean. Relaxing in her apartment and reading.

Mason was the type of man who thrived on adrenaline. Risked his life to help others. Trained hard and fought harder, and spent his down time playing sports with his friends.

He reached over and took her hand, and she felt electricity shoot straight through her.

He was an attractive man, no doubt, but something about Mason simultaneously sent heat coursing through her and shivers racing down her spine. She was electrified by his touch. And he couldn't seem to keep his hands off of her.

"I like knowing that you'll be here worrying about me. Maybe I shouldn't, maybe that's a cave man sort of mentality—the woman waiting back at home. But I love knowing that you care, sweetheart. I worry about you, too, when I'm not around. Why do you think I rushed over to your apartment last night?"

"This is crazy," she said, nervously pulling her hand away. "Everything just feels like it's happening so fast."

Mason's eyes were bright, warm—and seemed to see right through her. "Why's it crazy?" he asked, settling back into his own space. He leaned back on his elbows as he gazed at her, relaxed and casual.

How could he be so calm about something like this?

She'd confessed she worried about him when he was gone, and they'd barely started dating. Goodness, it had taken weeks just for her to agree to go out with him. They'd already been intimate together this morning—he'd made her come in her bed for goodness sakes.

A flush spread over her skin at the memory.

"Because—it just is. I always take things slowly when I meet someone."

"We've known each other for months," Mason pointed out. "Maybe we weren't dating then, but we've been texting. Talking at Anchors. Slowly getting to know one another. And hell—I want more of all this. I want you to spend time with my friends—and not just when you're working. I want to stay at your place again and have you at mine."

"You want me to stay over?"

Mason's eyes heated. "Hell yes. I want you in my space and in my life. I want you in my bed, Taylor. I want to explore your beautiful body and have you cry out my name. I want to claim you as mine."

"Wow, I just—I feel so overwhelmed."

"I don't mean to rush you, sweetheart. I'm just letting you know how I feel. Where I stand."

"It'll take some getting used to," she hedged. "I mean, you know I dated my ex for several years. He was always secretive about things—about his drinking, about his losing job after job. I almost don't know what to do with someone who has their act together."

"I'm sorry you dealt with all that—sorry he's still causing you problems. But I'm not like that. I've got a career in the Navy I'm dedicated to. I've got a circle of friends and teammates who literally would die for me—and vice versa. I don't play games—not with my career, not with my friends, and certainly not with the woman I'm dating."

"I appreciate that," she said, shifting on the blanket. "I like that you're open and honest. It's just a big adjustment for me." Her dress billowed slightly in the breeze, and Mason's gaze briefly swept to her bare legs.

Heat rose within her at his simple glance.

A crack of thunder in the distance sent her jumping, and Mason cursed.

The sky above them darkened even more as the wind blew in the storm clouds that had been off the coast. A couple of light rain drops began to fall, and Taylor hastily wrapped up the rest of her sandwich.

"It looks like the forecast was way off. The storm might blow over, but then we'll be soaking wet. My place isn't too far from here. How about we pack up and finish our picnic there? I'll drive you back to your apartment later on this evening."

"Okay, that sounds good," Taylor said, standing up on the blanket.

A big gust of wind blew her dress, and she shrieked as it billowed around her. "I'll get the food," Mason said, quickly gathering everything. He tucked everything into his backpack and grabbed the blanket as he stood, balling it up. He reached over for Taylor's hand, and then they were hurrying across the sand as the rain began to fall.

They were soaking wet by the time they got back to Mason's SUV, and Taylor began to laugh. "So much for beating the rain."

Her dress clung to her like a second skin, and Mason's gaze heated as it ran over her body. He impulsively ducked down and kissed her, sending a thrill shooting straight through her. He grabbed a towel from the back of his SUV, handing it to her as she climbed inside.

"Your seats will be soaked!" she protested.

"It's fine," he assured her.

A moment later he was rounding the car and climbing into the driver's seat, chuckling as the rain pounded down on the windshield. "So much for being suave and pulling off a nice picnic for our first date."

"Hey, you got a workout in," she joked. "Running back to your car was the most I've run in years."

"Well whatever you do, it works," he said. "You always look amazing."

"Walk," she said, towel-drying her hair. She dabbed at her chest with the now sopping wet towel. "I walk down the boardwalk. Running isn't really my thing."

"No problem there," he said with a chuckle. "I run because I have to for training. It's not exactly fun unless you're running through the rain with a beautiful woman."

She flushed as Mason started the engine.

"I have some dry clothes you can change into at my place," he said, glancing over at her. "They'll be way too big, but at least they'll be warm. Or I can take you home to get something if you'd prefer."

"I guess I can change into something of yours if you don't mind," she said shyly. Mason had to be a foot taller than her, but something about wearing clothing that was his, that had been flush against his skin, sounded appealing.

"All right. I kind of like the idea of you wearing my clothes," he said, his voice gruff.

He pulled onto the road, his windshield wipers swishing back and forth. Another loud crash of thunder sent her jumping in her seat. The heavens completely opened then, with rain pounding down on his SUV.

"I'm glad you have a large vehicle," she said as Mason carefully navigated the wet roads. "With some of these storms we get, I'm worried to drive alone through them in my small car."

"You've probably met some of the guys on the other SEAL team in Anchors," he said.

"Probably. It's tough to keep track of everyone, but there's definitely familiar faces in there every week."

"One of the guys, Mike, has a girlfriend named Kenley. Actually, I think they're engaged now. It's hard to keep track of everyone on their team. But anyway, Kenley's car ran off the road in a bad storm a year or so ago. Mike ended up finding her when no one else could."

"Wow, that's amazing. And horrible," Taylor added.

"Yeah, amazingly she wasn't hurt too badly, and her car was in one piece. She was stuck inside though and couldn't get out."

"You seem like you're all really close," she observed. She had her best friend Bailey of course but never a large circle of friends like Mason did.

"We are. But you'll get to know all of them more, too. We all look out for one another."

A few minutes later, Mason was pulling into the driveway of a townhouse not far from Little Creek. "Are you renting?" she asked, feeling slightly envious of all the space he must have. Her tiny apartment worked for her, but she'd love to have a bigger home someday to decorate with her photos.

"I bought it a few years ago," he said proudly.

"Consider me impressed."

He shrugged. "I get hazard duty a lot of the time, and there's not much I need. I saved up and was ready for my own place." He looked out the window at the pouring rain. "I guess we can make a run for it. I can go in and grab an umbrella if you want, but seeing as though we're already both soaking wet…."

"Let's run," she agreed.

"All right. I'll grab the food from the trunk and then come around to get you out."

Before she could protest, he was already opening the driver side door and circling the car. The hatch to the trunk closed as soon as he grabbed his backpack, and then Mason was opening her door. He helped her step down, the rain pouring down around them, and before she could say a word, he was scooping her up into his arms. He pushed the car door shut with his side as she clung to him, and then Mason was jogging up the front steps.

He typed in a few numbers on the keypad he had instead of a keyed lock, and then they were inside his foyer, Mason gently setting her down. His hands ran down her sides as she got her balance, as if he didn't want to let her go.

Her nipples pebbled beneath her dress, her chest rising and falling at Mason's closeness.

"I'm getting your hardwood floors all wet," she belatedly noticed as water dripped off her.

"It's fine," Mason said, his voice gruff. His wet tee shirt clung to his chest, and she could see his broad pectorals and the outline of his firm abs. He stepped out of his shoes, kicking them to the side, and then he ducked down and was kissing her. Softly at first and then more intensely.

She shivered at his touch, and his hands freely roamed her body.

Palming one breast. Wrapping around her waist.

He tasted of the ocean and something else darker and distinctly male.

His thumb grazed over one nipple through the wet cotton of her dress, and she softly moaned.

Gasped as one of his hands dropped to her thigh, teasing beneath the fabric. Clutching the fabric of her damp dress, his hands slowly dragged it up her thighs. "Let's get these wet clothes off," he said huskily, and then Mason was lifting her dress.

The fabric slid further up her thighs, revealing her lacy white panties. And then he was tugging it further up, over her breasts. She lifted her arms above her head as he growled in approval, and he tossed the dress to the floor as she stepped out of her sandals.

Mason stripped off his own wet shirt and then stepped closer to her once more, smelling of the ocean and soap and something else distinctly male. His hands slid up her ribcage as he pulled her closer, and she felt his arousal against her bare stomach. His fingers trailed over the cups of her bra and then slid under the straps, pulling them down her arms. He reached around her back and expertly undid the clasp, and she gasped as her bra fell away and cool air washed over her breasts.

"God. Taylor," he muttered, his gaze heating as he looked at her.

His hands slid over her bottom and then he lifted her into his muscular arms. Her legs locked around his waist as his fingers dug into her ass, his erection pressing against her core. He lifted her slightly, rocking her against him, and she moaned at the feeling of his hardness pressed against her folds.

He carried her down the hallway, her nipples rubbing against his bare chest as she clung to him. Somehow, despite the cool rain, Mason was impossibly warm. Coursing with heat and tension.

But it was nothing compared to the lust surging through her at his touch.

Every step he took nudged his cock against her panties, and she whimpered and moaned against him. Mason claimed her mouth in a searing kiss, even as droplets of water trailed down her back from her wet hair.

A moment later he was lying her down on his bed, pausing in front of her to admire her nearly naked body. Her legs dangled off the side of the bed as she lay gasping in front of him, wearing nothing but her white lacy panties. Mason undid his belt and pulled off his wet shorts, tossing them to the side.

Taylor giggled despite herself. "Your entire house will be soaking wet."

"Totally worth it," he said with a grin, his blue eyes heating as they eagerly slid over her. "And hell, Taylor, you are a sight to behold. I think I'll have this image of you lying on my bed, nearly naked, burned into my brain forever."

"Oh no," she protested, raising a hand to cover her eyes. "I'm soaking wet and probably look awful."

He lifted her hand and pinned it above her head, gazing down at her.

"You look amazing. Your damp hair around your flushed cheeks. Your perfect breasts with those round, rosy nipples. And your pussy covered by that sexy little scrap of fabric. I can't wait to explore you—all of you," he said with a growl. "I want to suck on your tits and tease you. Pull down those sinful little panties and taste your arousal. Eat out your pussy until you're screaming my name."

His lips met hers again, his erection tenting his boxer shorts. His tongue sought entrance to her mouth, and she parted her lips, letting him control their kiss. Claim all of her.

His tongue caressed hers, moving against it so wickedly, and she softly moaned into his mouth. Mason released the hand he'd pinned to the mattress and began making his way down her neck, kissing and nipping at her. His tongue flickered over one nipple as he moved lower still, causing her pussy to dampen, and she cried out as he sucked the taut bud into his mouth.

Mason's fingers trailed down her abdomen, his large hand splaying across her stomach. His thumb traced up her slit over her panties, and he lightly pressed against her clit, causing her to cry out for him. He briefly laved attention on her other breast as he softly rubbed her clit, leaving her moaning and writhing for him.

Needing more.

He finally kissed his way down her stomach, leaving her trembling. Thick fingers edged beneath the waist of her panties, and then he was tugging them down her legs. Parting her thighs for him.

He knelt on the floor before her, gripping both of her ankles. Lifting up both of her legs, he placed her feet on the edge of the bed and kept a firm hold around each ankle.

Holding her in place.

Baring her completely to his gaze.

She gasped as he edged closer, his broad shoulders spreading her thighs further apart.

And then his lips were softly kissing their way up one of her inner thighs.

She trembled at his touch, wanting, needing so much more. Arousal dampened her folds, and her clit throbbed. Suddenly his mouth was finally hovering over her, and he kissed her intimately, his mouth and tongue exploring her folds. She gasped as heat coursed through her, coiling in her belly and traveling lower still.

Her legs shook as he held them, and he draped them over his broad shoulders, his hands moving to her hips as he held her in place.

"Mason, oh God," she moaned.

She was spread out before him like a feast he was about to devour, helpless to his determination to pleasure her. He licked and suckled at her, teasing and gentle. His tongue lightly traced from her core up to her clit, and she gasped as it circled around her throbbing bud.

She fisted the sheets, arching up toward him. "Oh God, more. Mason, more!"

Mason growled with approval before lightly flickering his tongue over her clit again and again, pushing her higher and higher up to the precipice. She thrashed on the bed beneath him, held in place by his hands as much as her own lust. She would die if he stopped.

If she didn't come soon.

Nothing—no one—had ever driven her higher than this.

He continued his ministrations, expertly teasing her with his tongue, and she began to see stars.

Gasping, she cried out his name.

She was hovering on the edge of a cliff with no way to turn back. With no way to stop the onslaught of lust racing through her. Mason sucked her swollen bud into his mouth, and she exploded, screaming his name as she shot straight to ecstasy.

His tongue continued to lave at her, her legs spread wide over his shoulders, and her orgasm went on and on.

Mason eased up ever-so-slightly, kissing her clit softly as her sex throbbed. Her inner walls spasmed, clamping down around nothing. He licked her again, drinking up all of her juices, and she would've been embarrassed at how wet she was if she wasn't so completely sated. So incapable of thinking of anything but the pure pleasure coursing through her.

He turned his head and kissed her inner thigh again, before lifting her legs down off of his shoulders. They dangled off the bed once more, but she was too relaxed to even move. His fingers lightly ran up her inner thighs, making her shiver with delight.

"You taste fucking amazing," Mason said as he stood, gazing down at her bare breasts as he tugged down his boxers. His erection sprang out, thick and throbbing. "Hell, I could go down on you all night. Spent hours worshipping you."

She flushed as he turned and crossed over to his nightstand, his erection bobbing in front of him. His body was a sight to behold—nothing but pure masculinity. The muscles on his back bunched as he leaned down to grab a condom from the drawer, and he was back a second later, sheathing himself in front of her.

A thick vein traced up the underside of his shaft, and she tried not to gasp at how large he was.

"Are you ready for me, sweetheart?" he asked, his blue eyes sparking with arousal. He ran one hand up his shaft as if he couldn't hold back a moment longer.

"Yes, God yes," she murmured.

Mason edged forward, lifting her legs around his waist and pulling her even closer to the edge of the bed. The head of his cock briefly nudged against her clit, and she gasped, still swollen and throbbing from her screaming orgasm.

He nudged against her once, twice more, and then lined his cock up with her entrance before slowly pushing in, leaving her breathless.

She gasped as he inched in slowly, the exquisite pressure nearly too much to bear. Her inner walls stretched to accommodate him, and finally he bottomed out, balls deep inside of her. He held her in place a moment, staring at where their two bodies were joined together.

She hastened a look herself, and there was something erotic and sinful about this beautiful man taking her this way. Claiming her as his.

Muscles rippled across his abdomen, his jaw clenched in concentration, and Taylor realized he was holding back. Making sure she was ready to fully accommodate him. She thrust her hips lightly, encouraging him on.

"God, you feel so good. You're gripping me so tightly," he said through clenched teeth.

"Take me," she said.

He held her in place just a beat longer, impaled by his engorged shaft, and then he pulled slightly out and began thrusting. Taking her as his. Sending every single nerve ending throughout her body alight with pleasure.

The base of his cock rubbed up against her clit with every thrust, and he reached between them, rubbing his thumb softly over the swollen nub. She moaned and closed her eyes, too far lost in him to care about the sounds she was making. Mason began to take her harder, grunting as he pistoned in and out of her body. She began to climb again, and as his thumb moved faster over her clit as his cock filled her, she cried out his name.

Screamed as another orgasm came out of nowhere.

"Fuck!" Mason grunted as her inner walls clamped down tightly around him.

He hardened impossibly more, and then he was coming right along with her, thrusting in and out of her body as if she were made to be his.

Moments later he nearly collapsed on top of her, breathing hard from his own intense release. His lips brushed over her forehead, her eyelids, her lips, before he pulled out and collected her into his arms. The last thing she remembered was Mason tucking her into his bed, his large body curling around hers as they both fell fast asleep.

Chapter 11

"Holy shit," Bailey said the next day as Taylor recounted her date with Mason. "You went back to his place and slept with him? Hot damn, girl! How was he?"

Taylor blushed and took a sip of her chocolate milkshake. "Good—amazing. It makes me wonder why I wasted so much time with what's-his-name."

"Truth," Bailey said, brushing her blonde hair behind one ear, her tiny silver hoops glinting in the sunlight. "I told you months ago to break up with Eric when his drinking got worse and worse."

"I should've," Taylor agreed. "I just never realized what I was missing—both in and out of the bedroom, apparently."

"So, I guess a second date isn't out of the question."

Taylor giggled. "Nope. We haven't exactly set anything up yet though. Mason drove me home after dinner last night since he has to work today. We ended up just getting Chinese carryout. He was worried about leaving me alone at my apartment with Eric still lingering around."

"He's sweet," Bailey said. "And I'm worried, too. Showing up in the middle of the night at your place is escalating things to the nth degree. I mean before he claimed he wanted to talk or what not, but this? You don't barge into an ex-girlfriend's place at three a.m."

Taylor shuddered. "I haven't heard from him since. And Mason tried calling that jerk friend of his about my car."

"Which you still don't have," Bailey needlessly pointed out.

"He claims the part they need is coming this week. If it doesn't, I think Mason is ready to just have it towed somewhere else."

"Damn. He's hot, he's protective, he's a freaking Navy SEAL, and he's apparently amazing in bed. Lock that one down quick, girl."

"I don't think he's going anywhere. Some guys just want to get into your pants, but Mason? He wouldn't be showing up to get rid of Eric or calling about my car if he was just a one-night-stand kind of guy."

"Absolutely not. And the picnic on the beach for your first date? That's so romantic. Where can I find one of these SEALs?"

Taylor chuckled. "Come work at Anchors with me. The place is always filled with Navy men."

"That's a hell to the no," Bailey said with a laugh. "I'm done with waitressing—no offense."

"They have bartenders there, too," she said. "Imagine how much fun we'd have working together over there."

"I know, but the tips are awesome where I'm at, and I have the schedule I want. When you're new, you never get a say in your shifts. Besides, there's no need to change jobs. Not when my best friend can introduce me to her boyfriend's Navy buddies."

"What happened to that guy Bryan? I know you just started dating, but I thought it was going well."

"It's not going at all—he couldn't get it up."

Taylor nearly choked on her milkshake "It? As in you slept together?"

"Sleeping is all that happened. I did a little striptease for him, he took off his boxers, and nada. I was standing there in my sexy new lingerie, and he couldn't perform. Like at all."

"Well that's unexpected."

"To say the least. He said we'd try again another time."

"Try again?" Taylor asked with a giggle. "Like there's a chance his equipment won't work then either? Maybe he was nervous."

Bailey shrugged. "Let's just say that was the first and last striptease he's going to get from me. Aside from things in the bedroom not exactly working out, he started acting like he had all these other women wanting to date him."

"So what, you broke up?"

"I told him it wasn't working out. He left, and I took an amazing bubble bath. Alone."

"Well shoot. I thought we could double-date or something if things work out with Mason."

"They will," Bailey assured her. "And yes to the double date. Just let me know which one of those delicious-looking men you'll be introducing me to. I'll be wearing my sexy little lingerie beneath my outfit and ensure the night has a very happy ending."

"Bailey!" Taylor said in admonishment.

She grinned back, her eyes twinkling. "Okay, so maybe that'll be the second date. But bring me along when you're all getting together."

"Mason did mention they have bonfires on the beach sometimes."

"Excellent. I could snuggle up to a hard-bodied SEAL."

"You're relentless," Taylor said.

"And that's why you love me," Bailey finished. "So, what do you say? Shopping time?"

"Yep," Taylor said, grabbing her empty cup. "I need some new dresses for showing off to Mason."

"Then let's go do some damage to your credit card," Bailey said with a grin.

***

Mason grunted as he lifted the barbell above his head, Noah spotting him in the weight room. He fully extended his arms, lifting it higher and then brought it back down, his muscles rippling with exertion.

"Not too bad," Noah scoffed as he helped him put it onto the rack.

"Not too bad my ass," Mason said as he stood. "I'd love to see you do better."

"Easy fellas," Ryker said with a smirk as he sauntered over. "Don't get your panties in a twist. Let me show you how it's done."

"Guess we need a smaller weight then," Jacob quipped from where he was doing reps from across the room. The other men howled with laughter.

"Aw hell," Hunter said with a grin, swiping his

brow. "The rumor at Anchors the other night was that Ryker doesn't have a small anything. Amazing how your reputation proceeds you."

Mason smirked, his mind drifting as the others carried on around him.

He'd woken Taylor late yesterday afternoon and made love to her once more in his bed. They'd showered together afterwards, and he'd given her a clean tee shirt to wear while they ordered dinner. Her dress had eventually been air-dried in his dryer for the drive home, but there had been something sexy as hell about her walking around in his clothing.

The tee shirt had hung down to mid-thigh on her, but she wore the damn thing better than he ever had.

Her full breasts had pressed up against the soft cotton, and even though she'd smelled like his soap after their shower together, he loved that she smelled like him.

He'd claimed her as his own, kissed her entire body, and then showered and fed her.

Male pride surged through his chest at caring for his woman.

It had pained him to drop her off last night at her apartment, but he couldn't have her stuck at his place all day. PT had started bright and early, and driving her home first thing would've been just as bad.

"What are you smiling about?" Hunter asked him with a smirk.

"Just remembering my day with Taylor yesterday. She has the day off today, and I'm stuck here on base with you assholes."

"He's got it bad," Noah said with a grin. "When should we expect the invitations?"

"What invitations?" Colton asked as he sauntered

into the weight room.

Mason crossed his arms and leaned back against the wall. "Noah's giving up the Navy to become a wedding planner."

Colton smirked. "Another one bites the dust. Camila and I aren't engaged, so did you pop the question with Emma?"

"That would be a hell no," Hunter said. "Emma doesn't believe in marriage, and I'm not sure if I do either. Living in sin seems to suit us just fine."

Mason's gaze shifted back to Colton. "I took Taylor out yesterday, so in Noah's world, that's the equivalent of a walk down the aisle." He stood, striding over to spot Noah on the weights.

"Shit," Noah grunted. "I thought that's how we did things now. Haven't you been around the other team lately? Every last one of them has a woman. Even the CO, who I thought would never have a girlfriend, is dating Ice's sister."

Mason chuffed out a laugh. The Alpha SEAL leader's sister was a free spirit, completely the opposite of the hard-assed CO. "Wonders never cease. I can't say I expected Hunter to end up with a live-in girlfriend, but as soon as those two met in London, they couldn't keep their hands to themselves."

"Speaking of women, what's the update with Taylor? She's still got the ex who won't leave her alone?" Hunter asked.

Mason frowned, filling the rest of the team in on what had happened over the weekend. "I added all your numbers to her cell phone, just in case she can't reach me. Although she did finally file a police report when he showed up in the middle of the night."

"That's fucked up," Ryker said.

"Agreed. It sounds like the dude couldn't hold down a job since he was drinking all the time. Now he's fixated on her. They were together several years, so he seems to be having trouble letting her go."

"Some guys want what they can't have," Hunter said.

"Absolutely. And therein lies the problem."

Mason helped Noah put the weight back on the rack after he did a set of reps, his mind on the woman he'd spent all weekend focused on. It was crazy in some ways. He'd flirted with her for a long time at Anchors before ever even getting her number.

Something about being with her felt so fucking right though.

And when he'd had her in his arms yesterday—in his bed?

All thoughts of taking things slowly were gone in a flash. He wanted to deal with the problem of her ex, but he simply just wanted her, too.

In his life. In his bed.

When you know, you know, and while he didn't want to scare her with the intensity of his feelings, he knew neither of their lives would ever be the same.

Chapter 12

Taylor carried a tray of drinks across Anchors the next night, her gaze sweeping to the door every time it opened. She chastised herself for being so fixated on watching for Mason. For expecting him to come strolling in the front door every couple of minutes. They'd just spent hours together on Sunday. A romantic picnic on the beach, running through the rain together, making love back at his apartment.

And though she'd had the day off yesterday, with plenty of time to replay the weekend again and again in her mind, he was back on work. Busy with the guys on his team.

Mason was a freaking Navy SEAL. Those guys trained hard on base every single day. Drilled out on the water. Conducted scenarios and simulations she couldn't even imagine. It's not like he had a desk job where he could sit around and day dream.

Mason and his buddies usually came into Anchors

once a week or so for drinks, but it's not like he was here every night with his friends and hadn't shown up. Just because they'd slept together didn't mean he'd be here all the time. It didn't mean they were together. They still hadn't even made plans for another date yet. Mason had sent her a couple of flirty texts last night, but he was occupied at work. And rightfully so.

"You okay?" her friend Amy asked, pausing on her way across the restaurant with an empty tray in her hand.

"Oh yeah, I'm fine. Just distracted."

Amy shot her a knowing look. "So is a second date in the works?"

"Not yet," Taylor said with a smile. "Mason's been texting me though. You know how some guys follow that 'wait three days to contact the girl' line of thought? He's not like that at all, which is refreshing."

"I haven't seen them in here since Friday night."

"Nope," Taylor agreed, a tiny kernel of doubt seeping in. "They're busy with training and stuff on base."

"Oh yeah, I believe it. I just thought he'd be in here more now with you two dating or what not."

Taylor nodded, pressing her lips together. Amy didn't mean anything by that—she was just making an innocent comment. Taylor hated to admit that she'd had that exact same thought though. Wouldn't it be romantic for him to just show up out of the blue and surprise her? Drop by for a visit just to say hi? He was probably tired after a long day on base though. And he wasn't exactly her boyfriend.

Not really.

Although he had said they were dating. Why did

things have to be so complicated?

She blew out a sigh and carried the drinks to the table. A young group of guys was seated around it, and she couldn't help but wonder if Mason and his friends were like them years ago. They were all in their early twenties and flirted with every female in sight—including her.

Taylor got the distinct impression they'd take home any willing woman. They weren't after a relationship, they just wanted a warm body in bed with them. Goodness, probably not even for the whole night.

She took their food orders and then crossed the restaurant to put in their order. A couple seated at a table across the bar area gestured for her to come over, and she held up her hand, indicating she'd be there in a minute.

A deep male voice calling out her name had her turning in surprise, and she froze in place as she spotted Eric walking toward her.

He swayed slightly, and she could tell he'd been drinking again. He had several days' worth of stubble on his jaw and a rumpled shirt tucked into his jeans. He was nearly as tall as Mason but not quite as muscular.

That didn't stop her from wanting to back away as quickly as possible.

His hand landed on her upper arm, gripping it just a little too hard.

"Eric," she said, pulling away in surprise.

He frowned, looking puzzled that she'd backed away from him.

What had she seen in him all those years anyway? He was handsome, she supposed, when he was sober.

But he couldn't hold down a job. Couldn't even manage to get through an entire day without drinking.

"You weren't home," he said, stumbling slightly as he stepped closer. His breath reeked of alcohol, and she cringed.

"I'm busy working. You shouldn't be here."

"You don't need to work; I'll take care of you, baby. Come back home so we can be together."

She raised her eyebrows. "You don't have a job, Eric. The entire time we were together you were constantly getting a new job and then promptly getting fired a couple of months later. Besides, that doesn't even matter. We broke up. It's finished. Over. Go home to your own apartment and stay the hell away from mine."

"I just want you back, Tay." She cringed slightly at the nickname he'd given her. All of her friends called her Taylor, Mason included, but Eric insisted on shortening it. "I know I probably made some mistakes, but I miss you. I want you."

She cleared her throat. "I'm seeing someone else now."

He guffawed. "That dude that was there the other night? The Navy guy? He doesn't want you. Not for more than a couple of nights anyway. Those guys are with different women all the time. I've seen them in here myself. Ask anyone and they'll tell you."

Taylor glared at him, getting impatient. "You need to leave, Eric. We broke up a month ago, and I'm working. Go home."

A trace of anger flared in his dark eyes. "This is a bar, Tay. I have as much right to stay here as anyone. More so, even, since we were together for so long. I can order drinks and sit here all night if I want, then take you home with me afterwards."

"I filed a police report. You can't keep showing up at all hours of the day and night wanting to talk to me. Not when I told you it's over. How long were you waiting at my apartment the other day? Why'd you come back in the middle of the night?"

"I want you, baby. I miss you." He stepped closer, invading her space, and she tried to back away again but was trapped between the tables of the crowded bar area. Conversations continued on around her, music played, drinks flowed. But she was trapped. Stuck here in the middle of the bar with her ex.

He ducked lower, his lips hovering near her ear as his hand landed on her waist. His grip was like a vice, and she froze, her heart pounding. "I miss fucking you, Tay," he said, his hot breath on her ear making her squirm. "I miss your hot little pussy. Of having you in my bed every night and being able to fuck you anytime I want. My cock is hard as a rock right now. Let's go home and make up, baby. I'll make you scream my name until you can't take it anymore. I'll fuck you hard all night long and show you who your man is."

Taylor pulled back and slapped him across the face, shocked, drawing the the attention of some of the other patrons.

"Don't be that way, baby. I miss you."

"Are you okay, Miss?" a man seated at a nearby table asked as he rose to his feet. His fists were clenched, his gaze narrowed on them. The other men seated at his table had stopped eating and drinking to watch the situation unfolding.

Taylor glared at Eric, disgusted. "I'm fine. He was just leaving."

A spark of anger flared in Eric's dark eyes. "Tay, let's go home."

"No! You need to leave right now," she said, her hands shaking.

The guy standing at the table took a step forward, pointing a beefy finger at Eric. "You need to go. The lady just asked you to leave."

Eric's gaze swept from the man who'd stood up to the others seated at the table. He held his hands up in surrender, clearly outnumbered. "I'll catch you later, Tay." He turned and began walking out of the bar, but then glanced back over his shoulder. "Keep the bed warm for me, baby."

Taylor's mouth dropped open as tears pricked her eyes, and she turned and rushed toward the women's room, bursting into tears the moment she stepped inside. Maybe Mason was right. She did need a restraining order of some sort, because this was just going to escalate. Eric wasn't going to stop bothering her.

Maybe at first he'd shown up because he was lonely and wanted to talk, but now he was demanding that she come back to him.

That she come home with him.

Heck, maybe he'd never give up simply because he couldn't stand the fact that she was with someone else. It was so simple and twisted at the same time. They hadn't even slept together in months, Eric always too drunk each night to do much of anything. Yet the second he realized she was seeing someone new, he was taunting her. Telling her they needed to get back together.

Saying that he wanted to fuck her.

His crude words had been meant to shock her, to

humiliate her, and they'd done exactly that.

Maybe he hadn't shouted them loudly enough for the whole bar to hear, but they served as a reminder that she'd been with Eric for years. That he knew her body intimately. That his hands had been everywhere. Repeatedly.

He knew what it felt like to make love to her. He knew what it sounded like when she came.

Heated embarrassment washed over her.

Being with Mason had been amazing. Incredible. He'd been gentle and loving and determined to satisfy her again and again.

But the memories of being with Eric just left her sick to her stomach.

With trembling hands, she pulled out her cell phone. She briefly thought about calling the police but instead hit the call button when she saw Mason's name.

"Hey sweetheart, I'm just heading out of base. Are you at work?"

"Yeah," she said, her voice breaking

"What's wrong?" Mason asked, immediately on alert. "Are you okay? What happened?"

"Eric was here," she said, wiping away the tears streaming down her face. "I guess he went to my apartment first—I'm not sure. But he showed up ten minutes ago saying he missed me. Telling me to come home with him. Then right as he was leaving, he said that I needed to keep the bed warm for him."

"Son of a bitch," Mason muttered. A string of curses followed. "We need to file a restraining order. Having at least one police report of him trespassing is a start, but you need to document every time he shows up. Everywhere. Daytime, the middle of the night, your workplace. All of it. We can get security footage from your apartment and Anchors if we need to. Hell, we'll pull footage from the damn traffic cams. We'll tell the police all the times he's come over harassing you, and the way he threatened you. I swear to God, sweetheart, I won't let him touch one hair on your head."

"I know," she said, hastily swiping away the hot tears that continued to roll over her cheeks. Her breath hitched. "I know. I just—I'm scared."

"Hell, sweetheart, I'm on my way. Please don't cry. I'm just leaving base, already in my car, but I'm heading right over there."

"To Anchors?"

"Yes. He's not still there, is he?"

"No, he left. A group of guys at the bar saw him talking to me and asked if I was okay. I think they scared him off."

"He might be back later on," Mason said. "Let's talk to your manager, too, and see if they can keep him out. Once you have a restraining order in place, he'll be required by law to stay away. But we should talk to everyone working at Anchors to make sure he stays out."

"You're right. Shoot," she muttered, glancing over at the bathroom.

"What's wrong?"

"I'm working. I'm carrying around an order I took ten minutes ago—I was supposed to put the order in with the kitchen." She blew out an exasperated sigh. Glancing in the mirror above the sinks, she saw dark circles under her eyes from where her makeup had run.

So much for waterproof mascara.

"Well hell. Go to the manager and tell them what's going on. Give the order to someone else. As soon as I get there, we'll head for the police station. I'll be there in about twenty minutes."

"Okay."

"That reminds me, I talked to his friend Jake this morning. The asshole with the body shop. The part for your car is coming in today, so it should be ready for you to pick up by tomorrow afternoon. I'll go with you to get it."

"Well that's a relief."

The door to the women's room opened, and as two women walked in, she stepped aside and then exited, hurrying back toward the kitchen to turn in her order. "Listen, I have to get going. I'll see you soon."

"I'm on my way. If for some reason Eric shows up again, call 911. Don't waste time trying to talk to him. He sounds unhinged enough as it is."

"I will. Thanks Mason."

"I'll see you soon, sweetheart," he said, his voice gruff. "Be careful until I get there."

"Okay, I'll see you soon," she echoed, before ending the call and tucking her phone back into her back pocket. She swiped the remaining tears beneath her eyes and took a deep breath. Telling her manager about Eric was only the first step. The situation had already gotten completely out of hand.

Chapter 13

Mason parked in the fire lane at the corner of Anchors, jumping out of the car. He slammed the door shut, not even bothering with the alarm, and ran to the sidewalk. "You can't park there!" an older gentleman walking down Atlantic Avenue shouted, and Mason waved him off.

Can't park there his ass.

Taylor had been inside frightened and crying because of her asshole ex. A little thing like a ticket from the Virginia Beach PD wasn't enough to stop him from rushing to her.

Hell.

It was either that or double parking by the cars on the street. And then he'd be blocking traffic.

He shoved open the door and hurried in, not realizing he'd been holding his breath until he spotted Taylor coming back from the kitchen. Her dark hair was pulled back into a ponytail again, her eyes were slightly red from crying, and her face was pale. Her eyes lit up as soon as she spotted him, and then she was rushing across the restaurant, straight into his arms.

"Who-hoo!" a group of rowdy young sailors near them shouted as he lifted her into his arms.

Taylor wrapped her legs around his waist, clinging to him as she buried her face in his neck. Mason ran his hands over her back and hair, soothing her. Assuring himself that she was okay. She was safe. Her ex had scared her, yes, but she wasn't physically harmed.

He took a deep breath, inhaling her coconut and sunshine. Hell, the last time he'd been with her, she'd smelled like him. Like his soap and shampoo, his sheets.

His mouth had been all over her, his cock deep inside her.

And now his only concern was holding her until she stopped shaking.

Gently, he set her back on the ground so he could look into her eyes. "Thanks for coming," she whispered, swiping away a stray tear that appeared.

"Like I would be anywhere else? Your safety is my first priority. Always. Let's go talk to your manager. We'll see what he says and then call the police."

"I already talked to the manager. They've seen Eric around some other days, apparently. The bartender had to cut him off at one point. They're fine with telling him to leave when he shows up."

Mason nodded, clenching his jaw. His eyes raked over Taylor again. She had on her usual Anchors tee shirt, a pair of ripped-up jeans that were so popular with the women nowadays, and plain Converse chucks.

But damn.

She looked sexier than if she'd been in an evening gown—her jeans hugging her hips and ass. Her tee shirt just snug enough to show off her chest and remind him of what was underneath. Her smile when she looked at him was what really slayed him though.

She trusted him. Felt safe when he was near.

The way she'd sounded on the phone earlier had chilled him to the bone. She'd been crying. Scared. And Eric hadn't technically even done anything illegal. Saying you wanted someone in your bed wasn't exactly against the law.

But Taylor had been shaking when he'd arrived. And just knowing that that asshole wouldn't give up, wouldn't let her move on, had him seeing red.

"Do you have to finish your shift?" he asked in a low voice, his eyes meeting hers.

"No, they think I should go to the police, too. I explained why I hadn't shown up to work a couple of times—because Eric had been at my place. It's kind of a relief to get it all out in the open now. I was embarrassed before, because he kept coming over and wanting me there with him. Saying he needed me. I felt like I didn't have any control. But telling everyone here at work was liberating in a way. It's like I have more people watching out for me now."

"That's a good thing," Mason assured her. "And my team always has your back, too. If you couldn't have gotten ahold of me, you could've called any of the other guys. They'd have been here immediately."

"I understand," she said softly. The worried look in her eyes slayed him.

"Are you ready to go to the police station? Or do

you need to finish some things up here first?"

"No, we can head out," she said untying the half apron around her waist. "I just need to grab my purse and stuff from the back. I'll feel better getting my car back tomorrow. I just feel sort of helpless without it—like if Eric shows up or comes over, I can't leave."

"He's doing that intentionally," Mason said in a low voice, his gut churning. He didn't like that she didn't have transportation either. Eric could pretty easily guess she'd be at work or at home. "What exactly was wrong with it, anyway? Jake told me he needed to order a part. I'm starting to wonder if Eric did something to it."

"I don't know," Taylor said with a shrug. "It wouldn't start, and Eric happened to be over here. This was after it broke down on the side of the road that one time."

"How did his friend end up towing it anyway?"

"Eric called me around the time it broke down," she said, a look of recognition creeping over her face. "Actually, he'd shown up that day, too. Just to drop off some of my things that he still had, so I didn't think that much about it. This was before he kept coming over all the time. He called when I was on the side of the road with car trouble, and he assured me his friend would come and give me a tow. I was relieved actually, because I was scared. That bastard," she muttered.

Mason smirked despite himself.

"Don't laugh," she protested, lightly swatting his chest.

He captured her hand in his and held it against his chest for a moment, his large hand wrapping around hers. She flushed prettily, and he brought it to his mouth, brushing his lips across the back of it. "I'm not laughing at you," he assured her. "Well, just the fact that you called him a bastard. He's been manipulating you. I wouldn't put it past him to have messed with your car. And the fact that you were stranded on the side of the road because of it makes my blood boil."

"I was pretty freaked out," she admitted. "I was so glad his friend came to help me out, I didn't even question the cost."

"Hell, if I ever called and found out you were stranded, I'd pay for the damn tow truck myself if I couldn't get there."

"You wouldn't have to do that," she said, looking surprised.

"Of course I would. It's my job to take care of you."

"Mason, we just started dating."

"I know," he said, taking on a more serious tone. "And I plan to keep dating you. I'd do everything in my power to make sure you were safe."

"You're sweet," she said.

"There we go with you calling me sweet again. We can't let word get out about that, all right? What would the other guys say?"

She smiled up at him, making his heart pound in his chest. Jesus. You'd think he'd never been with a woman before. The way Taylor looked at him sometimes made his chest fill with pride though. He felt ten feet tall as he put his arm protectively around his shoulders.

"So, should we head to the police station now?"

"Absolutely. We'll fill a report, and then I'll take

you home. I have to be on base early for PT, but I can stay with you, if you don't mind my slipping out by five a.m. I'll make sure to lock up behind me."

"Okay, I like having you stay there."

"Me too, sweetheart. I know things have gotten off to a rocky start, given the situation, but hell. There's nothing I love more than being with you. Holding you in my arms when we sleep."

"Or don't sleep," she quipped.

Mason resisted the urge to groan. He didn't need to be thinking with his dick right now. He had his woman to protect. A police report to file. But once they got home for the night, he planned to have his hands all over her.

To make her come on his mouth and his cock.

To hold her so close she'd never be frightened again.

To make her forget about everything and everyone but him.

***

Two hours later, Mason and Taylor walked out of the police station hand-in-hand, and Mason's stomach rumbled.

Taylor giggled beside him, and without thought, he playfully bent down and swung her up into his arms. After two hours of talking to the detective, listening to Taylor recount every detail of the past few weeks, he was done. Done thinking about it. Done worrying about it.

Mason was exhausted from his day on base and starving, but at the moment, he wanted nothing more than just to hold Taylor in his arms.

"Mason, put me down!" she shrieked as he carried her to the car.

A police officer walking in chuckled, and Mason grinned.

"The officer inside the precinct said for you to be careful," he teased. "I'll stay the night and inspect every room in your apartment to make sure it's safe. After that, I'll kiss every square inch of your body with the same thoroughness."

Taylor squirmed against him as his cock hardened. The side of one of her breasts rubbed up against his chest, and he resisted the urge to groan.

He lightly set her down on her feet again, loving the smile that lit up her face. It had been a stressful couple of hours reporting everything to the police. Imagining how frightened she was every time Eric came over to her apartment. Although she'd told him about some of the times Eric had been coming over, he hadn't realized the extent of it.

Hell.

He'd been off on missions with his team while she was stuck in her apartment with her ex.

His blood boiled that she hadn't had anyone to turn to. Sure, she had her best friend that lived across town, but it's not like she could do much aside from offer Taylor a place to stay.

"Goodness, it's already after eight," Taylor said as she glanced at her phone. The sun was just beginning to sink lower in the sky, and Mason again thought how one of these days he'd love to be at the beach at sunrise with her. They'd have to hit up the west coast to see the sun sink over the Pacific, and Mason wasn't averse to that thought.

Damn.

When had he ever wanted to travel with a woman?

Usually taking his date back to his apartment was enough for him. But Taylor was someone he wanted a future with. He wanted to take her on vacation, take her home to meet his parents. They'd barely begun seeing each other, but somehow he just knew she was it for him.

"Want to get some carry out and eat at my place?" she asked, drawing his mind back to the present.

"Absolutely. I'm famished."

"Do you think Eric will show up?" she asked nervously.

"If he does, we'll call the detective. And 911. He probably thinks you're still at work though."

"Good point. That doesn't mean he won't be waiting around for when my shift ends."

Mason muttered under his breath, knowing she had a point. All the more reason for him to stay and ensure her safety. The fact that he wanted her in his arms all night was beside the point. An added benefit, perhaps, but his priority was her protection. "Let's get you home," he said huskily.

"Thanks again for coming tonight," Taylor said softly as he opened the passenger door of his SUV for her. "I know you were busy on base all day, but when Eric showed up at work, I was terrified. He seemed different somehow. Angrier. And when I told him that I was seeing someone, he didn't take it very well."

"Sweetheart, I was serious when I said I'd protect you. Yes, we've just started dating, but I'm not going to let some asshole scare me off. I'm definitely not going to let you deal with this on your own. If we get the restraining order and he keeps showing up, he could end up behind bars. Honestly, that would be a relief."

Taylor blew out a shaky breath. "I was hoping he'd get over it, get over me, but at this point, I just want him gone. If the police have to be involved, and he ends up in jail, then so be it. I'm done letting him control my life."

"I'm proud of you," Mason said. "I know it wasn't easy talking to your coworkers or going to the police. Hell, you were with the guy for years. He couldn't always have been such a jackass. But you're stronger than you know."

He grabbed the seatbelt and helped her buckle in, his hands lingering on her body.

"I can buckle myself in," she said with a small laugh.

"Humor me. I like being close to you, like touching you. I just want to make sure you're safe."

Her breath hitched as their eyes locked, and he ducked lower, his hand curling around the back of her neck as his mouth landed on hers. She tasted sweet, and he simply wanted to devour her. Taylor opened her mouth to his, and he deepened the kiss, loving the soft moan she made.

He kissed her a moment longer before reluctantly pulling back. "Let's get going before they come out and arrest me for public indecency or something."

"For a kiss?" she asked with a laugh.

"That was a hell of a kiss. And now I'm hard as a rock," he said, backing away and shutting the door. He winked at her from outside the window then turned away, willing his body to calm down as he circled the vehicle. He'd barely touched her, and his libido was roaring.

They needed to get home though. Eat. With the way his stomach was rumbling, he knew Taylor had to be starving as well.

All fantasies of claiming her beautiful body, of kissing her and pleasuring her would have to wait until later.

He opened the driver's side door and climbed in, groaning as he adjusted his half-erect cock.

Taylor giggled and licked her lips mischievously.

"What?" he asked with a chuckle. It was nice to see her relaxed, if only for the moment. She'd been scared at Anchors and stressed out at the police station. Even to see her smile for a few minutes filled his chest with pride. He wanted her to know he'd take care of her. Protect her. Satisfy her in bed and be there for every other part of her life, too.

"I like that I can do that to you," she said with a twinkle in her eye. "You always seem like you're so in command and control—I liked that I could make you feel that way."

"You liked making my cock so hard I could barely even walk?" he asked in a chocked voice.

"Mmm-hmm," she said innocently.

Mason muttered under his breath. If they weren't in the damn Virginia Beach PD parking lot, he'd be hauling her into his lap at this very moment. Tugging her jeans down, freeing his aching cock, and sinking into her silken walls. Thrusting up into her until she was panting and moaning and crying out his name.

He could barely keep it together as it was to drive her home. The way she'd licked her lips earlier made him imagine her mouth on him.

He wouldn't last a minute with her lips wrapped around his shaft.

Taylor was sweet, to be sure, but that hint of spice was what did him in. Just when he thought he'd figured her out, she'd surprise him in some way. Stripping off her top in bed. Or licking her lips and declaring she loved making him hard.

Holy hell.

She blushed like a schoolgirl sometimes but had an inner vixen that he adored.

"Should we get going?" she asked with a knowing smile.

"Absolutely." He started the engine and backed up, cursing as a car behind him honked.

He was off his game tonight. Totally distracted by the woman he was falling for. And since she still didn't have her car back, he sure the hell didn't need to be getting into an accident.

"What are you in the mood for?" he asked as he pulled out of the parking lot. "Pizza? Chinese?"

"I could go for some Mexican. I even picked up some beers at the store yesterday."

"For me?" Mason asked, keeping his eyes on the road.

"For you. Bailey drove me to the store and knew right away who they were for. No surprise really that my best friend knows me so well."

"Be still my heart," Mason quipped. "You love Mexican, bought me some beer, and are the prettiest woman I've ever seen. You better be careful, sweetheart."

"Why's that?" she asked with a laugh.

His eyes heated as he looked over at her. "Because I might not want to let you go."

Chapter 14

Taylor took a bite of her chicken taco, moaning in appreciation. The fresh salsa, cilantro, and avocado pieces atop the seasoned chicken were pure perfection. She took a swig of her beer and smiled as she caught Mason watching her.

"I thought you said you were a wine drinker."

"I am. Usually. I happen to love a beer with spicy Mexican though."

"Hoorah," Mason said, holding up his longneck before taking a swig. "I'll have to remember that."

She laughed, watching him inhale the rest of his food. She'd ordered two tacos plus homemade chips and guacamole for her dinner, but Mason had gone with a huge assortment of food. He took the last bite of his steak burrito and then grabbed one of the beef tacos he'd ordered. He still had an enchilada and his own order of chips and salsa.

"This food is fantastic. I can't believe I've been

stationed at Little Creek for years and never eaten there. How'd you find it?"

"It's kind of hole in the wall," Taylor admitted. "A tiny little place, but the food is amazing. We used to come here when I was a kid."

"I didn't know you were from here," Mason said, popping the cap off of his second beer. "Do you have family here?"

"No, my parents moved down to Florida—from one beach to another," she said with a wry smile. "They're happy down there with the other retired folks though."

"Any siblings?"

Her smile faltered. "I had a sister. Have a sister. She was killed in a car accident ten years ago. We were just teenagers then."

"Oh my God, I'm so sorry," Mason said, reaching over and taking her hand. "Were you close?"

She looked down at his hand holding hers, his thumb absently tracing small circles over her skin. Looking back up, his blue eyes were focused on her. Patiently waiting for her to collect her thoughts. "Yeah, we were close. Best friends. She was only a year older than me, so we did everything together. I know some siblings close in age don't get along, but for whatever reason, we always did. It feels like a million years ago now though. We were practically kids."

"What happened?" Mason asked quietly.

"A drunk driver hit her. She stayed out past curfew, and my parents were furious. I guess she figured she'd live dangerously for once. She was usually a rule-follower just like me. Didn't drink, didn't do drugs—none of that stuff. She was at a friend's house watching movies, and I was home sick. Maybe if I'd been with her, she would've come home on time. She left around midnight to sneak back in, and someone T-boned her in the intersection. A drunk driver with an alcohol level way over the legal limit. I saw photographs of the scene afterwards, and both cars were totaled. He didn't survive either, but my sister was innocent."

She sniffed, swiping away the tears that had begun to fall.

She hadn't told anyone that story in years. Bailey knew about her sister of course, and Eric had as well.

Ironic, to realize now how concerned Mason was that she was upset. Eric had nonchalantly commented that he was sorry but had been more concerned that she wanted a tattoo with Tessa's initials. Mason rose from his seat, taking the beer bottle she didn't even realize she had in a death grip. He set it aside as he knelt down in front of her, and then he was pulling her into his arms.

Holding her as she quietly cried.

"Shhh, I'm sorry, sweetheart. I've got you," he murmured, running one large hand down over her hair.

She sniffled again, relaxing into his warmth. This was the second time tonight she'd fallen apart in his arms, she realized. What must he think of her? Her whole life felt like it was in shambles at the moment.

Pulling back slightly, she looked right at Mason. He thumbed away a stray tear rolling down her cheek but stayed knelt beside her.

"I'm thinking of getting a tattoo of Tessa's initials," she confided. "Maybe just a small heart with 'TR' in the middle and the day that she died."

"You should do it," Mason said, his voice thick with emotion. "She was your sister and best friend. What a beautiful way to memorialize her."

"You really think I should? I don't have any tattoos."

"Absolutely. I love the idea."

Taylor huffed out a breath. "Yeah, me too. Eric was always against it. He said he didn't like tattoos on women."

"Eric was an asshole," Mason said immediately. "A controlling jerk. Maybe he wasn't physically abusive toward you, but trying to control your life was a different type of abusive."

"Yeah, I think you're right. And I'm really starting to wonder if he messed with my car, too. He was controlling in ways I didn't quite realize, and after we broke up, it's like the worst side of him finally came out."

Mason glanced at the clock on wall. "It's late, sweetheart. Let's make sure everything's locked up and get to bed."

"So you're really staying. I mean, I know you have to get up super early...."

"Hell yes, I'm staying. And not just because of your jackass ex. I love holding you in my arms. It feels right somehow."

"Yeah," she said, flushing slightly.

"Once again, I'm here and don't have any of my stuff though," he said with a chuckle.

"I've got a spare toothbrush," she said. "I don't think I have any clothes that would fit."

"It's fine," Mason assured her. "I can sleep in my boxers." His eyes heated as he looked at her. "I don't mind if you sleep in next-to-nothing either. Those lacy little panties you had on the other day were sexy as hell."

She blushed, letting him take her hand as they stood.

"I love the way you blush around me," he said, his voice gravel.

"It's embarrassing," she insisted.

"Wrong. It makes me imagine that flush all over your skin. It reminds me of making you come. Of hearing you cry out my name in bed, with my fingers or my mouth on you. Of my cock deep inside you. I love touching you. Pleasuring you. Making you forget about everything else but me."

Their leftovers suddenly forgotten, Mason was lifting her up into his strong arms. She wrapped her arms around his neck, her legs around his waist, and felt his erection nudging against her core. She moaned as he lightly thrust against her, letting her feel the delicious friction between them as he carried her down the hall to her bedroom.

The room was dark save for the moonlight coming in through the slatted blinds. But she felt safe. Content. Protected by the man she was falling for.

Laying her gently down on the bed, Mason was tugging down her jeans a moment later. Tossing her panties aside, his fingers trailing over her skin.

And then his mouth was upon her as he devoured her. His hands spread her thighs even wider apart, his fingers gripping her soft flesh as he held her in position. She rose quickly to the precipice, waves of pleasure buoying her up. Carrying her along.

His tongue trailed through her damp folds, laving against her swollen sex. Her clit throbbed for him, and then he was flicking his tongue lightly against it while she squealed in delight.

He circled her clit with the tip of his tongue as he edged two thick fingers inside her molten core. She moaned as he curled them just so, nudging against some secret spot inside. He began thrusting his fingers in and out, slowly driving her out of her mind. Finally, Mason took her clit between his lips, suckling her swollen bud, and then she was falling. Screaming his name. Coming over and over again.

Mason growled in approval as he kissed her sex, and she fluttered against his mouth, her orgasm never ending. Gently, he released her legs, kissing her one final time as she lay gasping. Fumbling around in the darkness, he muttered that he didn't have a condom.

"I'm clean," she whispered. "And on birth control."

"The Navy tests me all the time. I'm clean, too, sweetheart," he affirmed.

"Take me," she said, meeting his heated gaze in the dim light.

"You want me bare?" he asked, his voice gravel.

"Yes. Please Mason. I need you. I want to feel you deep inside me. Make love to me."

"With pleasure," he ground out. He pulled his erection free, not even bothering to push his pants all the way down, and lining himself up with her core, thrust into her in one long stroke. The heat from his thick length felt like he was branding her as his. Claiming her forever. Making her forget about anyone or anything except him.

He thrust into her again, groaning. She couldn't see where they were joined together in the darkness, only feel. He pumped into her again, moving slightly faster, and she gasped at the pure pleasure.

"You feel so good like this, Taylor. God, I can't hold back anymore. It's too much."

"Don't hold back," she said, grabbing his ass and pulling him even deeper inside her. "Come inside me. Take me, Mason."

His cock hardened impossibly more, and then with another quick thrust, he began pounding into her, leaving her gasping for breath. With one more thrust, he exploded, coating her with his hot seed. His short, rapid thrusts hit her in exactly the right spot, and suddenly she was coming again, too. Crying out as she clung to him.

His cock softened slightly, still buried deep within her walls, until finally he pulled free, ducking down for a lingering kiss.

A few minutes later, Mason was walking back from the bathroom with a warm washcloth.

"Let me take care of you," he said.

Much to her utter embarrassment, he cleaned her off, softly rubbing the material against her sex. Their eyes locked in the moonlight, and as his gaze softened, she knew she was lost to him.

Helplessly falling for him.

Her world had shifted completely off of its axis since they'd been together, and somehow, she knew it would never be the same again.

Chapter 15

Mason muttered a curse as he stood in the bullpen on base the next morning. He crossed his arms and gazed at the massive TV screen, dressed in his fatigues and combat boots, as his CO moved through a series of photographs of a terrorist camp they'd be infiltrating in the Middle East.

The rest of his teammates stood around him, eyes on the screen as well, ready to roll out.

"This is a new incident unfolding," his CO said, his voice grim. "We received this updated intel at oh-six-hundred this morning. We're going wheels up in one hour. The team will descend on the camp under the cover of nightfall and nab the target, then be back in the air almost immediately. The insurgent's wife is the American woman that defected to Syria. She was trying to get back into the U.S. last night but was arrested immediately upon arrival by U.S. Customs and Border Patrol. She was taken into custody and agreed to cooperate with the authorities."

"If she defected, what the hell is she doing back here trying to enter the U.S.?" Jacob asked, his eyes narrowing. "Was she involved in some sort of terror plot?"

"Affirmative," their CO said. He clicked through a new series of images. "She received training on building bombs and using suicide vests at the terrorist camp in Syria. It's believed that she was intending to detonate her suicide vest in the middle of Times Square."

"Holy shit," Hunter muttered.

"She's been detained and questioned by U.S. authorities. Fortunately, she had a change of heart after being caught. The threat of lifetime in prison can do that to a person. Plus, she was informed that she's six weeks pregnant. After agreeing to cooperate with U.S. authorities, she provided us with critical information on her husband, his training camp, and the whereabouts of others in the terror cell. The Pentagon wants him brought in immediately. When the terror plot doesn't go off as planned in two days, he might begin to question her loyalty. We're going to move in and grab him before the plot was ever supposed to occur."

Hunter nodded, clapping his hands together as he stood. "Let's do this. One terrorist mother fucker coming up on a platter. Let's deliver this bastard straight to Guantanamo."

Mason eyed him as they walked out of the bullpen. "You seem chipper this morning."

"Hell yeah," Hunter affirmed. "Let's get those bastards. That terror cell blew up a section of the market in London last week. Emma was in tears when that was all over the news. Now that we have confirmation of the location of the bastards responsible for it? I'm all in."

"Time to pay the price," Jacob agreed, falling in step beside them. "We don't usually get the location of a terror cell so quickly after an attack. This is fucking gold."

"Hell," Mason muttered. "I was supposed to help Taylor go get her car back today. I didn't even say goodbye to her this morning—just left her sleeping in her bed. I have to admit I didn't see this op coming."

"None of us did," Hunter agreed. "But we move in when needed. It's hard leaving your woman behind—I'm not going to lie. Our op down in Bogota was the first time I left Emma. Do you think I want her alone while I'm gone? But we do what we have to do."

"I know," Mason said, clenching his fists. "I'd just feel better if Taylor's asshole ex wasn't showing up all the damn time. I'll ask the other guys on the Alpha team to watch out for her while I'm gone. She has Ice's number for emergencies."

"She'll be okay," Hunter said. "We'll be back in what, thirty-six hours? I mean hell. She dated the guy for years, right? He's been bothering her for weeks. A day or two won't make much of a difference."

"I know," Mason said, tension coursing through him. "I just have a bad feeling."

"You're in love," Hunter said, ribbing him in the side. "Welcome to the club."

Jacob chuckled beside them. "That's one club I never intend to join."

Colton smirked as he followed them into the locker room to grab their gear. "Famous last words. I sure as shit didn't intend to fall for Camila. Hell, she was my target down in Florida. I was supposed to bug her luggage, not sleep with her."

"How'd you manage to get that job anyway?" Hunter asked with a chuckle.

"I was in the right place at the right time. Worked out to my advantage in this case. What if the notorious cartel leader in Bogota had a middle-aged son instead of a gorgeous, single daughter? We would've hauled ass down to Bogota with exactly zero intel."

Mason shook his head as he grabbed his gear. None of it was the same thing. Colton and Hunter weren't worried about leaving their women behind because they were safe. Rescued from the men after them. They'd left their homes and come to live here with their men.

Taylor might already live here in Virginia Beach, unlike when they'd met their women, but her ex was here, too. The last thing Mason wanted to do was fly across the Atlantic until this thing was solved.

Until he knew she'd be safe.

There wasn't a hell of a lot of options though, either.

He dialed Taylor's number, hoping she'd wake up. He'd left her alone in her bed this morning, brushing a chaste kiss across her forehead as she slept. She was used to a completely different schedule than him, working late hours and then sleeping in. Aside from that, it had been a stressful day yesterday. Her ex showing up, the police. As much as Mason would have loved to awaken her with heated kisses all over her body, taking the time to make love to her again, he had to be on base. And she deserved to get some rest.

Quickly typing, he sent her a text message since her phone kept going to voicemail.

We have an unexpected trip. Stay safe while I'm gone. Don't get your car without me. Xoxo Mason

It wasn't much, but what was he supposed to say? He couldn't exactly tell her where he was going. He sure the hell couldn't text the information. Groaning in frustration, he dropped his gear onto the ground, stuffing his phone into his bag.

The long flight across the Atlantic would give him plenty of time to think. And he had a feeling he'd be spending most of it worried about her.

***

Taylor yawned as she finally awoke several hours later, stretching her arms above her head. Her sheet brushed against her bare breasts, reminding her of how she'd slept naked wrapped in Mason's arms last night.

She was deliciously sore, her body well aware of how thoroughly Mason had claimed her. She blushed just thinking about screaming his name, about his hard cock thrusting into her again and again as she surrendered in ecstasy.

They'd awoken at some point in the middle of the night, his erection pressed up against her ass, and he'd gently parted her legs and made love to her again, holding her in his arms. His fingers had rubbed against her clit as he'd thrust into her, and she'd exploded again, crying out in his arms before they'd fallen back asleep, Mason's cock still buried inside her.

Glancing at the clock on her nightstand, she saw that it was already ten in the morning. Although she kept a late schedule with her work hours, this was sleeping late even for her. Grabbing her cell phone from the nightstand, her eyes scanned over the text from Mason.

An unexpected trip?

Confusion washed over her. She knew Mason and his friends got sent out when needed, but she'd assumed she'd have at least some notice that he'd be gone. She'd imagined making passionate love before he kissed her goodbye, promising to return soon.

A quick text from him after they'd made love the night before wasn't exactly the same thing. He hadn't even woken her up to say that he had to go.

Sighing, she stood up from her bed, her skin heating as she realized his scent was all over her skin. Mason always smelled of soap with a hint of spice, but there was something else erotically male as well. She wrapped her arms around herself, not wanting to let the moment go.

When she showered, she'd wash off his scent. The memory of him in her bed would be more distant, too. Sinking back down onto her bed, she swiped a few tears from her eyes.

She missed him.

She knew he'd be up early this morning to head onto base, but she'd assumed she'd see him again soon. Mason had told her himself he never knew how long he'd be gone when his team was sent out.

Would he be back in a few days? A week? Longer than that?

Rationalizing that she was being silly, she decided to go shower and dress. Her entire life didn't revolve around a man she'd gone out with a couple of times. It's not like they lived together or were married or something where she'd always be sure to see him before he left. When he packed for whatever mission he had to go on and rushed out the door.

They'd…slept together. Again. Sure, he cared about her, but she shouldn't make this into something it wasn't.

Her phone buzzed with an incoming call, and for a brief flash, she thought it was Mason. She tried to ignore the disappointment in her chest as she saw Bailey's name flash across the screen. She clutched the sheet to her chest, somehow feeling like she needed to cover herself even though her friend couldn't see her.

"Hi," she said, hating the slight waver of her voice.

"Hey hun, what's wrong? You sound sad."

Taylor laughed despite herself. "I said one word to you. How on Earth did you interpret that as sad?"

Bailey laughed. "I'm your best friend. So spill. What's going on?"

"Mason left," Taylor said.

"Left as in you broke up?" Bailey asked, sounding surprised.

"Left as in he had to for work. Deployed. Got sent out. Whatever you want to call it. He spent the night, and I knew he had to be on base early this morning. The next thing I know, I wake up to a text saying he'll be gone. I mean, do you think he purposefully didn't tell me he was leaving?"

"Oh, sweetie, no. He's not like that. Why would he go through all this trouble to help you deal with Eric only to sneak out?"

Taylor sighed. "He didn't exactly sneak out. He

told me last night that he had to be up early to be on base. I just assumed it was for training or something and that I'd see him later on." She went on to explain everything that had happened with Eric yesterday.

"Hell no," Bailey said. "Eric did not show up at Anchors and say that."

"Oh, he did," Taylor said miserably. "He wasn't acting like himself at all—he was angry. Mason came right away when I called him, but now I'm right back where I was before. Mason can't be around every second, and honestly, I'm surprised Eric didn't show up at my place last night."

"Maybe he was passed out drunk. Let's go have a girl's day," Bailey suggested. "Lunch, shopping, maybe a mani/pedi. I don't have to work until tonight."

"Yeah, me either. My shift is from seven until close."

"Perfect. How about if I swing by in an hour? We'll get you out of your apartment, have some girl time, and before you know it, you'll be off to work. You probably shouldn't be alone too much right now, what with the pending restraining order and stuff."

"I don't even know how that works exactly yet. We talked to a detective at the police station yesterday. He should be in touch to give me an update."

"All right, that's a good thing. If you don't hear from him, call them for updates. The squeaky wheel and all that. Get ready, and I'll come by to pick you up soon."

"Shoot. I should try to go pick up my car today, too."

"Is it ready?"

"It was supposed to be. Mason told me not to go without him, but I have no idea how long he'll be gone. I can't have everyone keep driving me around forever. It's already been a week and a half."

"Okay, let's go pick it up later on. It's at Eric's friend's place, right?"

"Yep. It's actually near the salon."

"Perfect. We'll get our mani/pedis and swing by before we have to head into work."

"All right, I'll call them to say we're coming later. Mason talked to Jake yesterday, so I'm assuming it should be all set. I'll see you soon." Taylor ended the call and set the phone back on her nightstand, taking another glance at the rumpled sheets on her bed.

How long would it be before Mason was back?

She had no idea how military wives or girlfriends handled frequent deployments. Mason didn't even really deploy—just got sent out on mission after mission. It's not like he'd been gone for six months or a year. There were plenty of local families who dealt with more than her.

They'd barely even begun dating.

She sighed as she stood, letting the sheet fall.

The slight ache in her core reminded her of just how intimate they'd been with one another. And even though he was gone, he'd be on her mind all day.

Chapter 16

Taylor giggled as Bailey pulled to a stop in front of her apartment building late that afternoon. "Oh my God, the look on that guy's face was priceless when you told him you'd cut off his balls if he didn't give us my car."

Bailey muttered under her breath, flipping her blonde hair over her shoulder, her hot pinks nails gleaming with fresh polish. "Yeah, well, it didn't do much good. We still don't have it. If I knew how to operate that damn lift thing, I would've taken it down myself."

"It wouldn't have done much good if they're still fixing it. Then again, maybe Jake left it up there on purpose. Mason said he was pissed as hell when he called him. Mason told him we were going to come get my car, and Jake wouldn't know Mason got sent out of the country. He probably left it up there just to mess with him."

"I wouldn't put it past him," Bailey said dryly. "Are you sure I can't give you a ride to Anchors for your shift?"

"No, but thanks, hun. One of the other waitresses, Amy, is coming by to pick me up."

"All right, if you're sure. Maybe you should call that detective and see what he says about them holding your car at the shop forever. Since Jake is friends with Eric, maybe there's something they can do."

"God, I hope so. This is getting ridiculous. I'll call him tomorrow first thing. I need to get ready for work, and if the police want me to come back now to file a separate report, I'll be late. I'm not sure there's anything illegal about a car shop fixing my car though. Even if they are friends with Eric."

"We'll figure it out. Thanks again for lunch."

"No worries. Thanks for driving me around all day." Taylor climbed out of the car and shut the passenger door, waving goodbye as Bailey drove away. Her own nails shone with pale pink polish. It had been refreshing to spend the day with her best friend. Lunch overlooking the ocean, strolling along some of the shops near the boardwalk, and then relaxing at the nail salon had been just what she needed to get her mind off of everything.

Pulling her keys from her purse, she climbed the stairs to her apartment. The flip-flops she'd worn for her pedicure slapped on every step. It was relatively quiet at this time of day, with most of the other residents still at work for their nine-to-five jobs.

She slid the key into the lock of her apartment and twisted the knob, pushing the door open.

She froze as soon as she walked in, her keys falling to the ground as Eric staggered toward her. The door automatically shut behind her with a loud thud.

"Tay, baby," he slurred. "I've been waiting for you all day." His hands wrapped around her waist, his large body towering over hers, and he planted a sloppy kiss on her lips as she tried to push him away.

He tasted of alcohol and fast food, and she pushed harder at his chest, trapped between the closed door and him, until he finally released her. "How'd you get in here?" she asked angrily. "You have no right to come barging into my apartment. And you sure the hell have no right to kiss me. I'm calling the police."

He grabbed her forearm, surprisingly strong despite being inebriated. She tried to yank away from him, and his fingers tightened around her, pulling her into her living room. "Don't be like that, baby. I talked to the super. Told her I accidentally locked myself out. Luckily, she remembered me since we dated for three years. She walked upstairs with me and let me in herself. Where've you been anyway? I've been waiting here for hours. Hope you don't mind that I drank a few of your beers."

Wrenching her arm free, she pulled back from him, putting a few steps between them. "None of your damn business. How I spend my time and who I spend it with has absolutely nothing to do with you."

"I miss you, baby. I told you that the other night at Anchors. I miss having you beside me in bed. I miss that sweet pussy of yours."

"You need to leave right now or I'm calling the police."

Eric's expression turned cold. "Where's your phone, Tay? You're not calling anybody. Give me your purse."

She clutched her purse tightly, his eyes following the movement. He yanked it free from her hands, carelessly tossing it across the room.

"Where's that Navy guy you've been fucking? I thought he'd be here with you right now. Stripping you bare. Licking your pussy." He laughed harshly, pulling his own phone from his back pocket. "I got some good footage of you two. I have to admit, I didn't realize you were such a whore. We dated a month before you'd have sex with me. You barely even know him and let him fuck you. That hurt, Tay. I shouldn't have had to watch that."

Her cheeks flamed as waves of embarrassment and humiliation washed over her, and she crossed her arms, shaking. Trying to hold in her emotions. "You're lying. You don't have a damn thing."

Eric unlocked his phone, swiping an app on the screen and pulling up some grainy video footage. He held it up, and Taylor wanted to vomit as she watched footage from a few days ago of her pulling off her camisole that first morning she'd been with Mason. Her bare breasts were on display as she straddled him, and moments later, she was crying out in pleasure.

"Give me that!" she yelled, reaching up as Eric chuckled and held the phone out of her reach. "Where the hell did you get that?"

"I've got plenty of videos of you two. I bugged your bedroom. I get to watch you walk around naked as you undress every night. I like to see those perky breasts bounce as you move. That gorgeous pussy of yours. Your ass as you bend over and slip on your sexy little panties."

Taylor covered her mouth with her hand, bile

rising in the back of her throat. He'd been watching her. Invading her privacy. Seeing her intimate with another man. What had Eric done with those videos? Had he shown his friends? Posted them online for the entire world to see?

"That's right, baby. I like watching you. You're mine. I love seeing your beautiful body. And I needed to see why you suddenly thought you were too good for me after three years. Why you picked that dumb fuck over me."

"You're a goddamn drunk, Eric!" she seethed, gasping in shook as he smacked her across the face. She lifted a hand to her cheek, the sting resonating through her. Tears smarted in her eyes.

"You know, I don't really like sharing you, but since your new boyfriend's not here right now, I thought we'd have a little fun tonight."

"I'm not sleeping with you," she said, her voice shaking.

He grabbed her arm, his bloodshot eyes raking over her body. "We need one last night together for old time's sake. Then maybe I'll let him have you back."

"No," she said, her voice trembling.

She took a step back, breaking free from his grip, and then turned. Ran toward her door in her flip-flops. Eric grabbed her from behind, hauling her up into his arms as he covered her mouth with one large hand.

She kicked and fought him, her sandals flying off, her arms restrained by his. He tightened his grip and carried her toward her bedroom, stumbling slightly along the way. "Don't be like this, Tay. We were good together."

She tried to cry out, his hand muffling the sound.

Eric was bigger and stronger than her, but maybe she could hold him off until he passed out. Hadn't that been what had happened every other night he'd shown up? He reeked of alcohol, started slurring his words after she let him into her apartment, then passed out cold.

He'd already said he'd had a few of her beers. And that was just while he was here. He'd probably been drinking all day long.

"Do you promise not to scream?" he asked, his lips at her ear. She cringed. "The cameras I've set up are on right now. I don't want to hurt you, baby. Don't make me do something that I'll regret. I need you. I just want your pussy one more time. I want to enjoy what's mine. Let's go to bed, enjoy each other, and maybe I'll give you the copies of the videos tomorrow."

Tears smarted her eyes as she bobbed her head up and down, agreeing not to yell.

He slid her down his body, one hand still covering her mouth, and set her back on the floor. His hand freely moved over her, clumsily fondling her breasts as she tried not to gag. "Shh, Tay," he said, staggering again as he moved her toward her bed.

Her cell phone was still in her purse out in the living room. She had exactly zero ways of contacting Mason. Of calling for help.

Her friend Amy was supposed to come pick her up soon for work. Hopefully if Taylor didn't answer the door or her phone, she'd realize something was wrong. Call the police. Notify someone.

She shuddered and gasped, realizing she had absolutely no idea when Mason would return. If Amy didn't realize something was wrong, would anyone? What if Eric didn't let her go? She'd flaked out on work so many times lately, they might not think anything of it if she didn't show.

Finally releasing her from his grip, Eric's bloodshot eyes bore into hers.

"How much have you had to drink?" she asked, her heart pounding in her chest.

"A couple of beers. Plus some vodka. It was only like half of the bottle though. Come to bed with me, baby. I need you. Give me what I want, and I'll give you the videos tomorrow."

Shuddering as Eric's fingers wrapped around her upper arm, she moved with him onto her bed. He stripped off his shirt, swaying slightly again. She didn't think he'd actually hurt her, but he'd changed so much from the guy she'd once fallen for, she wasn't sure about anything anymore. If she could just convince him to talk for a while, maybe he'd pass out and she'd be okay.

She could lie there in bed until she was sure he was out cold.

Pray he was too inebriated to force her.

Then sneak out when he was unaware, calling the police from outside.

"Come lie down with me, Eric," she said, her voice shaking. "I want you to hold me first. Please? Then I'll do whatever you want."

"I am a little woozy," he said, struggling to crawl toward her. Finally, he collapsed at her side and wrapped his large body around her, his chest to her back.

She'd have to burn her sheets after this.

This morning they'd smelled of Mason. Of their

lovemaking the night before.

And now they were tainted with her ex.

Nervously, her eyes tracked around her bedroom, wondering where the camera was. He'd had a close-up video of her, but was the camera zoomed in? Had they been watching the mirror image of it?

Maybe it was on the other side of the bed.

The weight of Eric's arms around her chest and waist felt like a vice. His entire body surrounded her. Held her. She squirmed against him, trying to edge away, and he tightened his grip. "Don't forget I have cameras in here, baby. I'll know if you leave. I'll come find you. Let's just rest for a few minutes, and then you can strip for me. Let me fuck you a couple of times." His words slurred more, and she squeezed her eyes shut.

Biting her lip to hold back her tears, Taylor lay stiffly in bed with Eric. She counted to one hundred. Two hundred.

Eric's soft snore finally filled the room, and she shakily released her breath.

It felt like an eternity had passed, but it couldn't have been more than ten minutes.

After several attempts, she lifted his heavy arm off of her, feeling it fall away. He didn't move. Didn't alter his breathing. Didn't say a word.

Inching toward the edge of the bed, so as not to shake it, she finally slid off, crawling across the floor barefoot in her jeans and tee shirt. She didn't think he'd wake up and see her, but why take any chances? She paused halfway across the room, listening for any movement. Afraid to look back.

Finally, she stood when she reached the hallway, ready to run for her purse and call 911.

A loud knock at the front door sent her leaping back in fright.

Chapter 17

Mason's gaze swept the perimeter of the camp in Syria through his night vision goggles, the scope of his weapon trained on the lone guard outside. The night air was still, save for the rest of his SEAL team members quietly moving into position.

"All right team, move in!" Hunter's voice quietly commanded over the headset.

Mason jogged forward in the darkness alongside Hunter, fifty feet away from the compound. The guard jerked his head in surprise at the red dot on his chest, fumbling for his weapon, and then a muffled shot sounded.

The guard slumped over. "One guard down. The north end is clear," Hunter said, his voice cool.

"Roger that. We've entered the south end of the compound," Ryker said over their headsets. "No guards in sight. We scaled the wall and are moving toward the center."

"Roger. See you fellas there," Hunter said.

Mason and Hunter moved quietly forward, the rest

of the camp sleeping. They passed two supply buildings on the left, weapons and ammunition piled in the open doorway. Whatever training occurred here was clearly a large-scale operation. Mason wondered why only one guard was outside the front of the compound. Hopefully it wasn't an ambush.

"Drone surveillance shows four men guarding the main building where the leader is located," Noah said. "I've got eyes on it now and only see three."

"The fourth guard is twenty feet away taking a leak," Ryker said. "I've got him in sight."

A quiet shot came over the headset, and Mason clenched his jaw, waiting for someone to hear it. For more insurgents to come running. The three guards at the center of the compound came into view. He could see slight movement in the distance where Ryker and Noah were quietly moving forward.

"There's no one approaching from outside the camp," Colton said. "I've been sweeping the entire area, and we're in the clear. Jacob and I are ready to roll out after we secure the package."

"Then let's grab this mofo and get the hell out of Dodge," Hunter said.

Shooting erupted as the three guards spotted them in the cover of night, and Ryker and Noah took them out from behind. Mason ran forward toward the door to the building, quick despite the heavy gear and Kevlar vest he wore.

The target appeared in the doorway, looking confused. Mason lunged for him, tackling him to the ground. Shouts erupted around them, and then Ryker and Noah deployed smoke bombs and flash bangs to confuse the insurgents.

Hunter hauled the terrorist to his feet, he and

Mason each gripping one of the man's arms as they dragged him, barefoot, back through the compound.

Their two Humvees rolled into sight, and then they were tossing him into the back, climbing in. Ryker and Noah came running behind them, hopping into the second vehicle. Smoke rose through the air in the background, looking hazy even through their night vision goggles.

Hunter spoke quietly into his headset. "Target is secured. ETA is fifteen minutes."

They received a confirmation over their comm channel.

Mason huffed out a sigh of relief as they sped through the night. Adrenaline surged through him, and he felt damn near ready to take on the entire world. Worry had niggled at the back of his mind since they'd landed in Syria, and for the first time of his career, he found himself wishing he had a regular job.

The type of thing where he didn't have to leave at a moment's notice, worrying about the woman he'd left at home.

The type of job where he could call up his woman. Send her a text. Hear her voice.

He'd never heard back from Taylor after he'd texted her that he'd be gone, although he figured she was still sound asleep by the time they'd gone wheels up.

He wished like hell he'd gotten a chance to actually talk to her. The Delta team was incommunicado with the rest of the world while out on an op, and it killed him that he couldn't check in on her. Make sure she was okay.

Tell her he'd be back soon.

The sooner they were in the air on a return flight across the Atlantic, the better he'd feel.

***

Taylor ran to the corner of the parking lot of her apartment complex as she heard sirens in the distance. As soon as Amy had shown up to give her a ride, the women had rushed down the stairs.

Amy had called the police, but Taylor had been so scared she'd kept running, wanting to get as much distance as possible between the building and her.

"Taylor!" her friend shouted. "The police are on the way!"

Taylor saw Amy standing near her car, glancing at the stairwell.

Part of her expected Eric to come racing down any minute, but maybe he was still passed out drunk in her bed.

Although a part of her felt guilty for abandoning her friend, Amy could've run, too. She'd taken one look at Taylor's frightened face and called the police immediately. Followed her down the stairs but paused at the bottom to talk to the 911 dispatcher.

Taylor huffed out a breath, scanning the lot.

Cars were pulling in as they arrived home from work, and it was crazy how it seemed so normal out here when she'd been trapped in her own apartment. When Eric had been waiting for her and refused to leave.

A rustle behind her in the trees had her turning, and then a man was beside her, holding a cloth over her face as she struggled. She tried to scream, but whatever chemical was on it was too strong.

She slumped over as the world faded to blackness.

***

Taylor awoke on a hard, concrete floor, the air inexplicably smelling of gasoline and oil. She was cold, scared, and nauseous, and she hesitantly pushed herself up to a sitting position, trying not to vomit. Her eyes slowly began to adjust to the darkness, and she heard a car engine outside.

Squinting, as if that would somehow help her see where she was in the darkness, she looked around.

Where had Eric taken her?

How had he gotten downstairs in her apartment building to come after her? Hadn't he still been passed out on her bed? She should've seen him in the stairwell. Crossing the parking lot. Coming toward her.

It made no sense.

A light suddenly flicking on overhead had her shielding her eyes. Heavy footsteps treaded across the room, and she looked up.

Eric's friend Jake stood towering over her, his arms crossed, a smirk across his face.

"Where's Eric?" she croaked.

"Arrested, probably. I watched the police come into your bedroom. They dragged him out of bed and took him away in handcuffs."

"You were…watching?" Confusion washed over her. Worry churned through her. Had Jake been in there, too?

"It was quite a show. As soon as I saw you sneaking out of your bedroom while Eric was passed out, I knew I had to come get you for myself."

Awareness suddenly blossomed within her.

The cameras Eric had set up in her room.

The videos.

If Jake had seen the police come in and arrest Eric, then had he seen her all the other times, too? Eric hadn't just secretly recorded her, he'd set up a live feed. Let his friend and who knows who else watch her in her bedroom.

She turned and vomited on the concrete floor, listening to him cross the room. The strong smell of gasoline in the air was making her nausea even worse. Jake handed her a paper towel and bottle of water, and she took them with shaking hands, wiping her mouth.

Staring at the full bottle of water.

"Eric set up a feed," he confirmed. She looked back up at him. "He owes me money. A hell of a lot, actually. He can't hold down a job to save his life, so I've been helping him out. When he still hadn't paid me back after you guys broke up, he said that I could watch you, too. I saw you walking around naked and with that boyfriend of yours. Watched him screw you in your bed. The thing is, I'm ready for the real thing."

Scrambling to her feet, she backed away from Jake.

The concrete was cold beneath her feet. She shivered as he stalked closer.

"Since I haven't heard from that Navy SEALs of yours about your car, I'm guessing he's not around. He wasn't there earlier to stop Eric from coming in. Lucky me."

Her gaze swept around the room, taking in the inside of the body shop. The cars and tools lying around. The oil stains on the ground. The windows.

The door, which felt like it might as well be a million miles away.

How long had it been since she'd run from Eric? How long had she been here?

"You kidnapped me!" she accused him. "You're just as bad as Eric. Worse even."

"Maybe I just brought you here to get your car back," he said with a sneer. "Isn't that what you wanted?"

"By knocking me out and taking me against my will? You're crazy! Give me the keys to my car, and I'm leaving," she said, hating the stutter in her voice.

Jake's gaze slid over her, and he scrubbed a hand across his stubble.

"Where's that tough guy boyfriend of yours now? The one who wanted to make me leave when I picked up Eric's sorry ass from your apartment building?"

Taylor cleared her throat, ignoring his question. "Give me the keys."

Jake aggressively moved closer to her, and Taylor took a step back, icy cold dread snaking through her. "What was that?" she asked as she heard a car door shut.

"Just one of my guys leaving. The shop is closing up for the night. No matter. We haven't exactly discussed payment yet."

"Eric didn't tell me how much I owed you, so just let me know, and I'll head out. I'll send you the money for the car."

"He didn't tell you the new arrangement? You're the payment, sweetheart." His voice was low. Quiet. Like he was trying not to spook her. He was the predator and she was the prey.

"What?" she asked, her heart beating rapidly.

"You're my payment," he repeated, stepping closer. Trapping her. One large hand wrapped around her hip, holding her in place as his other slid up her ribcage. Gripping her tightly. He pressed against her, his erection nudging against her stomach, and she screamed.

"Shhh," he whispered, covering her mouth with one hand. Squeezing so she couldn't move her head from his grip. "We're closed for the weekend. No one is around to hear you."

She trembled as he ducked down, his teeth grazing her neck. "I won't hurt you. I'll go nice and slow," he said, taking his hand from her mouth.

"No," she said, hating the way her voice shook with that one word.

"We have all night," he said. "I'll take you slow, up against the wall, and then maybe bend you over one of the cars and have you from behind. Maybe I'll call one of my guys to join us. You can suck me off later to finish."

His hands edged under her shirt, and she screamed, pushing against him and kicking him in the shin.

One large hand covered her mouth again as he shoved her back against the wall, and then suddenly the door burst open, Mason standing there, eyes blazing.

"Get the fuck off of her," he demanded, his voice low and deadly.

"Hey now, man," Jake said, easing slightly off of her. "We were just having a little fun."

"Wrong fucking answer," Mason said, moving toward him.

Jake backed away from her in haste now, realizing

his error.

She gasped in surprise as she saw two other men moving quietly into the room. They didn't look like the guys Mason was usually with at Anchors, and she wondered if they were from a different group of SEALs on base.

Before she could utter a word, the biggest man with ice blue eyes was tackling Jake from behind, taking him to the ground. Mason moved toward her, pulling her into his arms. The other man called 911, but Taylor shook and cried in Mason's arms, letting the soothing sound of his voice drown out everything else around her.

"I'm here, now, sweetheart. Shh. You're safe now."

Chapter 18

Taylor gasped as she awoke the next morning, sunlight streaming in through the windows. Her heartrate slowed as she realized she was safe in Mason's bed. Nestled in his arms.

Mason's arms tightened around her, and her breathing slowed back down as she felt his solid body next to hers. As she relaxed against his warmth.

"You're safe, sweetheart. You're safe. We're at my apartment. Eric and Jake are in jail."

"Oh God," she whispered, a tear rolling down her cheek. "I was having a nightmare. Reliving everything."

"No one can get you here," he assured her, nuzzling against her neck. "They've both been arrested, and I'm right here. I'll never let anything happen to you."

"How did you find me earlier? With the police and the chaos and my crying hysterically on the way to the hospital, I never even asked."

"When we got back to Little Creek, the Alpha team was already there. Someone from the Virginia Beach PD had contacted Ice. Patrick," he clarified. "I guess your waitress friend told them about me. That you were dating a Navy SEAL. The entire police department was looking for you when you disappeared from your apartment complex, but when Patrick said Eric had been arrested, I knew it was probably his friend Jake that had taken you."

"But how?"

Mason shrugged. "Just a hunch. He was at your place that one night to pick up Eric, and he just seemed unhinged. Plus, he was still holding onto your car for some reason. Most people want to get paid and move on to the next vehicle if they own an autobody shop. He seemed intent on keeping it there."

"He's as crazy as Eric," she said, shuddering.

"Maybe even more so. As soon as Patrick told me you were missing, I was rushing out to my SUV to go get you. Patrick and another man from the Alpha team came with me while the rest of my team debriefed on our mission. It wasn't exactly standard procedure to leave base like that right after an op, but my CO understood why I had to go. No one there could've stopped me."

"I was so scared," she said. "And when you came through that door, I couldn't believe it. I thought I was dreaming at first."

"I'm sorry I wasn't there sooner."

"Ugh, and I thought they'd never let me leave the hospital. God, I just feel…gross," she admitted. "Like I can't wash this day off me soon enough."

Mason chuckled slightly beside her. "We didn't get a full night's sleep. Aren't you exhausted? We can go back to bed for a few hours. I have some time off since we just got back."

"No, I just want to shower and wash Eric and Jake and everyone else off of me."

Mason stiffened beside her but rose and followed her into his bathroom. "They didn't—" he broke off, the expression on his face grim.

"No," she assured him. "Eric passed out drunk in my bed. And Jake—well God, I can only imagine what would've happened if you didn't come in right then. But you saved me," she assured him. "You got there in time."

He nodded, then turned on the water as steam began to fill the room. He took a deep breath, the tension slowly leaving his posture. "I never would've forgiven myself if they'd harmed you," he admitted. "I couldn't get to you fast enough. I just couldn't imagine anything happening to you."

"Thank you for finding me," she whispered.

"I'll always come for you, sweetheart. I'm just sorry I wasn't there to begin with."

"You were doing your job," she assured him. "Saving the world. But now I just need you here with me."

"You have me," he assured her.

Hastily, she took off her clothing, tossing it into a pile in the corner. Mason stripped as well, joining her a moment later in the shower.

He held her trembling body to his as the hot water poured down over them. She rested her head against his chest, loving the feel of his large hands running over her hair and back. Of his hard, muscled body holding her close. Of his lips brushing over the top of her head.

"Will you come with me to get my tattoo?" she asked suddenly as he held her to him.

Looking up, she met his blue gaze.

"Of course," he said. "Whenever you want to go."

"I realized once again how short life really is when Jake kidnapped me. My sister's been gone for ten years. It's hard to believe, but it feels like both yesterday and a lifetime ago. I want that heart tattoo with my sister's initials. I'm not going to wait around for the perfect time. I just want to go ahead and do it. To live my life with no regrets."

"Where are you going to get it?" he asked.

"Right here," she said, pulling away and pointing to her hip. "Just a small heart, but it's important to me."

His hand came to a rest on her waist, his thumb rubbing over the skin of her hip where she'd pointed. "To me, too," he said. "Because I want you happy. Safe. I love you, Taylor," he said, his voice thick. "I almost lost you, but I'm never letting you go."

"I love you, too, Mason," she said, her voice breaking. "Make love to me," she whispered.

"Are you sure? You've been through so much."

"I'm sure. I need you," she said, watching as his cock hardened. "I want you."

His hands reverently ran over her breasts, his fingers brushing over her nipples. They tightened beneath his touch, and he ducked lower, kissing her, as he gently backed her against the cool tile. His hand slid between them, parting her lower lips, and then she could feel his fingers sliding through her arousal-dampened folds.

"Hell, you're wet," he said, his voice gruff.

"For you," she whispered. "Only for you."

He stroked her sex, ensuring she was ready for him, and she whimpered and moaned as his fingers lightly brushed over her clit. He kissed her again, rubbing her gently, and before long she was gasping for breath.

Mason lifted her into his arms, his thick length running between her swollen folds as she wrapped her legs around his waist.

He lined himself up with her entrance, and then he was thrusting into her. Claiming her. Marking her forever as his.

The water from the shower washed over their skin, and with the cool tile at her back and the heat of Mason's hard body against her front, her senses were overwhelmed. His chest rubbed against her sensitive nipples, and his heavy cock stretched her completely, stroking her inner walls.

His hands slid to her ass, his fingers digging into her flesh, and then he was lifting her up and down as he took her. She cried out, clinging to him, as he took complete control of their lovemaking.

She couldn't move at all, he held her so tightly, and she didn't care.

She wanted him, needed him.

Was desperate for more.

Mason's cock hardened impossibly more, and with a series of short, hard thrusts, he had her screaming his name. Clinging to him as he lifted her up and down his rigid shaft. Drawing every last ounce of pleasure from her.

Mason stiffened, and with one last thrust, came inside her, shouting as he found his own release.

His seed coated her inner walls as she spasmed around him, milking his thick length.

He pressed her against the cool tile as he kissed her deeply, his cock still buried deep inside her.

"I love you, sweetheart," he said, tenderness in his eyes.

"I love you more."

THE END

Author's Note

Thank you for reading RESCUED BY A SEAL! We got our first real glimpse of Mason in Hunter's story, TEMPTED BY A SEAL, and I've been eager to write about him ever since.

Mason's a typical Navy SEAL, swaggering with muscles and bravado, and I liked pairing him with the demure Taylor. She's somewhat shy around him at first but isn't afraid to go after what she wants. The idea that they've been casually flirting for a while let me start off their story with a bang. She didn't expect for him to end up in her bed right away, but they had an immediate attraction to one another and couldn't keep away from each other if they tried to.

If you have a chance, please leave a quick review. It makes a huge different to indie authors like myself!

Make sure you sign up for my newsletter so you never miss out on a new release. I'm planning on Noah's book next, title still TBD.

As always, thank you for joining me on this writing adventure. I wouldn't be here without you!

xoxo,
Makenna

About the Author

USA Today Bestselling Author Makenna Jameison writes sizzling romantic suspense, including the addictive Alpha SEALs series.

Makenna loves the beach, strong coffee, red wine, and traveling. She lives in Washington DC with her husband and two daughters.

Visit www.makennajameison.com to discover your next great read.

Made in the USA
Columbia, SC
06 July 2025